She swallowed. "Like I said. Talk is cheap."

He smiled hungrily. "And like I said, I'm a man of action."

Then he leaned in and captured her mouth, not giving her a chance to stifle the moan that immediately rose in her throat. He wrapped his arms around her, and his hands stroked her back at the same time his tongue stroked every inch of her mouth.

She had long ago decided his kisses were unique, full of passion and capable of inciting lust. But she was also discovering that each time they kissed she encountered something else. This kiss was tapping in to her emotions and she was fighting like hell to keep them under tight control as far as Galen was concerned. This was all a game to him. Not for her. For her, it was about finding herself in more ways than one. Discovering her past and making headway into her future.

He deepened the kiss and she felt his hands move downward to cup her backside and pull her more fully against him. She groaned again when she felt his hardness press into her at a place that was already tingling with longing. Unfamiliar sensations were floating around in her stomach and she was drenched even more in potent desire.

Then he suddenly broke off the kiss and took a step back. She watched him lick his lips with enjoyment before he thrust his hands into his jeans pockets, looked at her and asked, "Did I make my point?"

Oh, he'd made it, all right, but she'd never admit it to him.

Books by Brenda Jackson

BRENDA JACKSON

is a die "heart" romantic who married her childhood sweetheart and still proudly wears the "going steady" ring he gave her when she was fifteen. Because Brenda has always believed in the power of love, her stories always have happy endings. In her real-life love story, Brenda and her husband of thirty-six years, Gerald, live in Jacksonville, Florida, and have two sons.

A *New York Times* bestselling author of more than fifty romance titles, Brenda is a recent retiree who worked thirty-seven years in management at a major insurance company. She divides her time between family, writing and traveling with Gerald. You may write Brenda at P.O. Box 28267, Jacksonville, Florida 32226, by e-mail at WriterBJackson@aol.com, or visit her Web site at www.brendajackson.net.

NEW YORK TIMES AND USA TODAY BESTSELLING AUTHOR

BRENDA
JACKSON

HIDDEN PLEASURES

To the love of my life, Gerald Jackson, Sr.

This year marks my fifteenth anniversary as a published author
and I want to thank all of you for your support.

To my readers who have been with me since my first book,
this seventy-fifth book is especially for you.

To my good friend and classmate Valeria Stirrup Jenkins of
the Chloe Agency Finishing and Modeling School in Memphis,
Tennessee, for her feedback on proper etiquette and manners.
Thanks for your help. It was truly appreciated.

Hear thou, my son, and be wise, and guide thine heart in the way.
—*Proverbs* 23:19

 KIMANI PRESS™

ISBN-13: 978-0-373-86164-4

HIDDEN PLEASURES

Copyright © 2010 by Brenda Streater Jackson

www.kimanipress.com

Printed in U.S.A.

Recycling programs
for this product may
not exist in your area.

Dear Reader,

This is my seventy-fifth book and I am proud to present it to you!

When I introduced the Steeles with Chance's story four years ago, little did I know that I would be writing beyond Donovan's story. But the more I wrote about that family, the more I knew I had to tell you about their cousins—those other Steeles who live in Phoenix. They are the ones you will get to know as the "Bad News Steeles."

There are six brothers and the oldest of the bunch is Galen Steele, a man after any woman's heart with no intention of letting any woman after his. Galen and his five brothers are convinced they will use their playa cards forever. But little do they know I have a surprise for each of them.

Join me in getting to know the Phoenix Steeles and enjoy reading how I sprinkle my love dust on each of their resistant hearts. In *Hidden Pleasures,* Galen wants Brittany Thrasher as another notch on his bedpost and makes her an offer he knows she can't refuse. At first it seems as if everything is going according to plan, but then fate steps in and Galen discovers the hard way that some things are just meant to be.

Thank you for making the Steeles a very special family. I look forward to bringing you more books of endless love and red-hot passion.

Happy reading!

Brenda Jackson

THE STEELE FAMILY OF PHOENIX
Family Tree

Drew Steele and Eden Tyson Steele

| Galen[+1] | Tyson | Eli | Jonas | Mercury | Gannon |

NOTE –

Drew Steele is first cousin to the fathers of Chance, Sebastian, Morgan, Donovan, Vanessa, Taylor and Cheyenne

1. *Hidden Pleasures*

KEY:

( ) – denotes a spouse

+ number – denotes title of book for that couple's story

Chapter 1

"Holy crap!" Galen Steele muttered as he turned away from the bank of elevators and raced for the stairways of the Ritz-Carlton Hotel in Manhattan. A high school soccer team was checking out and filling all the elevators going down to the lobby. Galen could not be late for this wedding. His cousin Donovan would kill him if he were.

All the other groomsmen had left for the church a good thirty minutes ago, but he'd lagged behind when a woman he'd met at the bar last night had unexpectedly knocked on his hotel room door just when he was about to walk out. Not one to turn down a booty call, he'd thought he could make it quick. He had no idea Tina What's-Her-Name didn't believe in a quickie. A smile split his lips as he recalled how she'd made it worth his while.

And now he was late. He'd heard of weddings being held up for the bride or the groom, but never for a groomsman.

He vividly remembered Donovan's warning last night at the bachelor party. His cousin, who'd been engaged two months shy of a year, had made it clear that he'd waited long enough for his wedding day and he intended for it to go off without a hitch. And that meant he wanted all twenty of his groomsmen to be at the church on time. As he spoke, he'd looked directly at Galen and his five brothers—not so affectionately known as the "Bad News Steeles from Phoenix."

Hell, it wasn't Galen's fault that his father, Drew Steele, had actually gotten run out of Charlotte over thirty years ago by a bunch of women out for blood— namely his. Drew's reputation as a skirt chaser was legendary, and although the old man had finally settled down with one woman, his six sons had been cursed with his testosterone-driven genes. Galen, Tyson, Eli, Jonas, Mercury and Gannon didn't know how to say no to a willing woman. And if she wasn't willing, they had the seductive powers to not only get her in a willing mood, but to push her right over the top. Or let her stay on the bottom, depending upon her favorite position.

Galen glanced at his watch again as he reached the main floor. Hurrying toward the revolving doors, he prayed a taxi would be available. This was New York

City, the Big Apple, and yellow cabs were supposed to be all over the place, right?

He smiled. One was pulling up as soon as he exited the hotel and he ran toward it, thinking he might be on time to the wedding after all.

Not waiting to be assisted by a bellman, he opened the cab's door, slid in the seat and was about to direct the driver to the church when he felt a tap on his shoulder. He looked up and his gaze collided with a face he could only define as gut-grippingly beautiful. Eyes the color of caramel, naturally arched brows, a cute little nose and a pair of too-luscious lips.

The beauty he'd finally gotten out of his room less than ten minutes ago had nothing on this woman. It was like comparing apples to oranges. Both were good fruit, but one was sweeter.

He found his voice to speak. "Yes?"

"This is my cab."

He couldn't help but grin when he asked, "You own it?"

Her frown gave him a warning. It also gave him one hell of a hard-on. "No, I don't own it, but I called for it. It's here to take me to the airport. I have a flight to catch."

"And I have a wedding to attend and I'm late."

She crossed her arms over her chest, and the shapeliest pair of breasts he'd ever seen pressed tight against her blouse. The sight of them made his mouth water. "Sorry, but your lack of planning does not constitute an emergency on my part," she said in a haughty voice.

"The proper thing for you to have done was to allow yourself ample time to reach your destination."

"Well, I didn't and as much I've enjoyed chatting with you, I have to go." He regretted saying so, because he would love to spend more time with her.

She dropped her arms and arched her shoulders. Once again his attention was drawn to her breasts. "This is my cab!"

"It was your cab, lady, and I really do have to go." He turned his attention to the driver and said, "I need to get to the Dayspring Baptist Church in Harlem in less than twenty minutes."

The driver shook his head, reluctant to move. "I don't know, man," he said with a deep Jamaican accent. "I was called to take a lady to the airport."

Galen took out his wallet, pulled out a hundred-dollar bill and offered it to the guy. "I'm down to nineteen minutes now."

The man almost snatched the bill out of Galen's hand and shot the woman an apologetic look. "Sorry, miss, I have a large family to feed. I'll call in and have another cab sent for you."

Satisfied, Galen reached over to close the door, but the woman—the sinfully beautiful but very angry woman—was blocking the way. He tilted his head back and looked up at her. "Do you mind?"

"Yes, I do mind. You have to be the rudest man I've ever met. Someone needs to teach you some manners."

He smiled. "You're probably right, but not today. Some other time, perhaps."

She glared at him as she moved out of the way, but not before saying, "And for heaven's sake, will you please zip up your pants."

He glanced down. "Oops." He quickly slid up his zipper before closing the door.

The cab pulled away then and he couldn't resist glancing back through the window at the woman they'd left at the curb. She was not a happy camper. In fact she looked downright furious. And he should give a damn why? Because he *had* behaved like an ill-mannered brute, which was not his typical behavior, especially when it came to beautiful women. It was definitely not the impression he would want to leave with one. If he'd had the time he would have charmed her right out of her panties and bra. It was the Steele way.

Oh, well. You win some and you lose some. And he'd much preferred losing her than his behind, and there was no doubt in his mind that Donovan would kick that very part of his anatomy all over New York if he was late for his wedding.

"I now pronounce you man and wife. Donovan, you may kiss your bride."

Donovan Steele didn't waste time pulling his wife into his arms and giving her a kiss many probably thought was rather long. And if that wasn't bad enough, when he'd finally pulled his mouth from hers, he whispered, "I love you, sweetheart."

Natalie Ford Steele smiled up at her husband and said, "And I love you."

And then she was swept up into her husband's arms and carried out of the church.

Galen swallowed to keep from gagging as he watched the entire scene. Even though Natalie was a nice-looking woman, a real beauty, he'd still had a hard time believing that Donovan had decided to hang up his bachelor shoes and take a wife. Donovan's reputation as a womanizer was legendary; in fact, he'd been so infamous in Charlotte that there were some who thought he was one of Drew Steele's sons instead of a cousin. Galen figured Charlotte wouldn't be the same without a bachelor Steele to keep things lively. Maybe he ought to consider leaving Phoenix and moving east.

He kicked that idea out of his mind real quick. His older Steele cousins in Charlotte would probably give him a job in their Steele Manufacturing Company. He much preferred remaining in Phoenix doing what he loved, which some people thought was trivial.

And his father topped that list of critics. Drew Steele believed that a man was supposed to get up at seven o'clock, Monday through Friday, and work at some job until at least five. It had taken Drew a long time to buy into the Principles According to Galen Steele, which said that a man was supposed to work smarter, not harder. That was why at the age of thirty-four Galen was a multibillionaire and was still building an empire, while working less than twenty hours a week and having fun at what he did.

Fourteen years ago while attending the University of Phoenix, pursuing a degree in engineering, he and his two roommates decided to do something to make money, something different than what their friends were doing—like selling their blood or their sperm. So they began creating video games. After their games became a hit on campus, they formed a business and by the time they graduated from college two years later, they were millionaires. The three of them were still partners today.

Their business, the SID Corporation, was represented by three CEOs, Galen Steele, Eric Ingram and Wesley Duval. Their only employees were their art team. He, Eric and Wesley shared duties as game designers and programmers and leased a suite in an exclusive area of Phoenix's business district for appearances' sake and as a tax write-off. They preferred designing their games right in the garage of their homes. Simple. Easy. Shrewd.

He shook his head. He and his brothers had inherited the old man's penchant for women, but they'd been born to excel. Drew's expectations for his six sons had been high, and all of them had become successful in their own right.

Seeing the other groomsmen move forward, Galen brought his attention back to the ceremony in time to stay on cue and file out with the rest of the wedding party. He took the arm of his partner, Laurie, one of Natalie's friends from college. She was pretty—and she was also very much married.

Outside in the perfect June day, he couldn't help but chuckle as he checked out the faces of his brothers and a number of Donovan's still-single friends. They had stood up there and witnessed the entire ceremony and they looked as if they were in shock. Galen understood how they felt. There wasn't a woman alive who'd make him consider tying the knot. He got shivers just thinking about it.

"You barely made it."

Galen came out of his reverie to glance over at two of his brothers, Tyson and Gannon. "Doesn't matter, Tyson. I made it," he said, smiling. "With a minute to spare."

"Should we ask why you were almost late?" Gannon asked with a curious look on his face.

Galen chuckled. He was the oldest and at twenty-nine Gannon was the youngest. Galen knew he was his youngest brother's hero and because of that he tried walking a straight-and-narrow path. Doing the role-model thing wasn't always easy, especially when you were the offspring of the infamous Drew Steele. But on occasion Galen liked pulling his youngest brother's leg. Like now.

"I'll be glad to tell you why I was almost late," Galen said, leaning close to his brothers as if what he had to say was for their ears only.

"I got caught up in a foursome and lost track of the time," he lied. And just so they would know what he meant, he said, "It was me and three women in my hotel room. Get the picture?"

"No kidding?" Gannon said, easily impressed.

Tyson rolled his eyes. "Yes, he's full of it, Gannon. Don't believe a word he says. It might have been one woman, but it wasn't three."

Galen could only smile. There were only eleven months' difference in his and Tyson's ages. A lot of people thought they were twins, but they were as different as night and day. Dr. Tyson Steele tended to be too serious at times.

"Tell him the truth, Galen, or Gannon is going to go around believing you're superhuman or something," Tyson said.

"All right." He gave Gannon his serious look. "There were two women. I took care of one and the other one got away," Galen said, thinking of the woman whose cab he'd been forced to hijack. He could still see the anger on her gorgeous face, especially the fire that had lit a striking pair of eyes.

"Was she good-looking?" Gannon had to ask.

Galen lifted a brow. "Who?"

"The one who got away."

Galen couldn't help but smile. "She was more than good-looking. The woman was absolutely stunning."

"Damn, man. And you let her get away?" Gannon looked clearly disappointed.

"It was either that or get my behind kicked by Donovan if I was late for his wedding."

"Okay, everyone, let's go back inside the church for pictures," the wedding director said, interrupting their conversation. "Then we'll return to the Ritz-Carlton for the reception."

Galen's thoughts shifted back to the woman. The one who got away. Like he'd told Gannon, she was more than good-looking and for some reason he could not get her out of his mind.

And at that moment he thought he'd give just about anything to see her again.

Brittany Thrasher tucked a loose strand of hair behind her ear after bringing her car to a stop in front of her house. It was nice to be back home after attending that seminar in New York.

A few minutes later she was walking through her front door wheeling her luggage behind her. The first thing she planned to do was strip off her clothes in deference to the Tampa heat that flirted with the hundred-degree mark.

She looked at the stack of envelopes on the table and couldn't help but appreciate her neighbor and friend Jennifer Barren for coming over every day to get her mail and water her plants. This was Brittany's busiest travel time of the year. As CEO of her own business, Etiquette Matters, she and her ten employees traveled all over the country teaching the basics of proper etiquette to businesses, schools and interested groups. Last week her students consisted of a group of NFL players who'd been invited to the White House for dinner.

Kicking off her shoes, she went to her bedroom and her mind went to the man in New York, the one who'd had the audacity to take her cab from right under her nose. And with his pants unzipped. He hadn't seemed the least bit embarrassed when she'd brought it to his attention. The jerk.

She shook her head. Another thing she remembered about him other than the open zipper was his eyes. He had Smokey Robinson eyes, a mossy shade of green that would have taken her breath away had she not been so angry. The man had no manners, which was a real turnoff. She would love to have him as a student for just one day in Etiquette Matters. She would all but shove good manners down his throat. In a gracious and congenial way, of course.

She flipped through the stack of envelopes, sorting out the junk mail that needed to be trashed. One envelope in particular caught her attention. The handwriting on it was so elegant, she'd give just about anything to have that kind of penmanship.

The envelope had no return address, but the postal stamp indicated it had been sent from Phoenix. She didn't know a soul in Phoenix and it was one of the few places she'd never visited. Using her mail opener, she opened the letter and her eyes connected to words that had her gaping in shock.

Ms. Thrasher,
I have reason to believe you are the daughter I gave up for adoption twenty-eight years ago.

Chapter 2

Six months later

"Will any of my sons ever marry?"

Galen refused to look up from reading the documents that were spread out on his desk. He didn't have to glance at Eden Tyson Steele to know she was on a roll. Ever since Donovan's wedding, his mother had been swept away by wishful thinking. She had witnessed the ceremony, heard the wedding music and seen how happy the bride and groom were. Since then she'd felt something was missing in her life, especially because Galen's kinfolk in Charlotte could now claim that all the North Carolina Steeles, both male and female, had gotten hitched.

He'd gotten a call earlier from Mercury warning him that their mother was making house calls to each of her sons. Her message was consistent and pretty damn clear. She wanted daughters-in-law. She wasn't pushing for grandbabies yet, but the brothers figured that craving wouldn't be long. First she had to work on getting them married.

"Galen?"

He breathed out a deep sigh. There was no way he could ignore her question any longer. Besides, he figured that the sooner he gave her an answer, the quicker she would move on to the next son.

He glanced up and gazed into eyes identical to his and those of his five brothers. They might have Drew Steele's features and most of his genes, but their eyes belonged to Eden Steele all the way. And Drew would be the first to admit that it had been Eden's eyes that had captured his attention and then his heart. "Yes, Mom?"

"Will any of you ever marry?"

He fought back a smile because he knew for his mother this was not an amusing moment. She was as serious as a heart attack whenever she broached the subject of her sons' marital status.

Galen leaned back in his chair and gave her his direct attention, which he felt she deserved, even if she was asking him something he'd rather not address again. "I can't speak for everyone else, but my answer to your question is no. I don't ever plan to marry."

Her expression indicated his response had been one

she hadn't wanted to hear. Again. "How can you say that, Galen?"

"Easily."

Seeing her agitation, he went on to say, "Look, Mom, maybe saying I'll never marry is laying it on rather thick, so let's just say it's not in my immediate future. Dad was almost forty when the two of you married, and everyone had given up on the idea he'd ever settle down and stop chasing skirts. So maybe there's hope for me yet."

He couldn't help but smile. What he'd said sounded good and should hold her for a while, but with the scowl on her face, he wasn't so sure. His mother was a beautiful woman and he could see how Drew Steele had taken one look at her and decided she was the best thing since gingerbread. There was a ten-year difference in their ages and according to Drew, the former Eden Tyson, a fashion model whose face graced a number of magazines worldwide, had made him work hard for her hand. And when they'd married, Drew had known his womanizing days were over and that Eden would be the only woman for him for the rest of his life.

Galen doubted such a woman existed for him. He had yet to meet one who could knock him off his feet... unless it was to make him fall flat on his back in their bed. He enjoyed women. He enjoyed making love to them. He enjoyed whispering sweet nothings in their ears. There was not one out there he would sniff behind other than to relieve the ache behind his zipper. What could he say? He was one of Drew's boys.

Most people in Phoenix either knew or had heard

about "those" Steele boys. While he was in high school, most mothers had tried keeping their daughters behind lock and key. It never worked. Chances were those he missed out on had fallen for the likes of Tyson, Eli, Jonas, Mercury or Gannon. No female was safe from that lethal Steele charm.

That lethal Steele charm...

Too bad he hadn't had the time to lay it on that woman in New York. The same woman he couldn't get out of his mind. When they'd gotten back to the hotel for the reception, he'd actually glanced around for her, hoping that perhaps she'd change her mind about leaving. He'd even gone so far as to wish that perhaps she'd missed her flight and had to come back. No such luck. But just for him to hope that much bad luck on anyone proved what an impact the woman had made on his senses.

"You and your brothers are not your father, Galen."

"No, but we are his sons," he said, holding his mother's gaze. "Dad didn't marry until he found that special woman, so I'd say the same will hold true with the six of us."

"And I hope when she comes along, the six of you won't screw things up."

He chuckled. "Like Dad almost did?" Of course he'd heard the story about how their father had refused to accept his fate and ended up pushing Eden away. By the time he'd come to his senses, she had left the country to do a photo shoot somewhere in Paris. Panicked that he had lost her forever, he had tracked her down and asked her to marry him. To some the story might sound romantic, but to Galen it was a good display of common sense on his father's part. His mother was world-class.

"So, Mom, where's your next stop?" he asked, throwing out the hint that their little talk had come to a close.

She sighed in resignation and tossed back the hair from her face. "I guess I'll drop by and see Tyson. This is his day off from the hospital."

Galen smiled. "You might want to call first. He probably has company." Usually any day off for Tyson meant a day spent in bed with some woman.

His mother made a face before waving her hand at his words. "Whatever," she said it in that I-don't-care-what-I-catch-him-doing voice.

He stood and came around his desk to give her a hug. "You do know that I love you and enjoy your visits, don't you, Mom?"

His mother sighed. "I won't give up hope on any of you, especially you because you're the oldest."

He lifted a brow and wondered what that was supposed to mean. She would have it easier marrying Gannon off than him. Galen had been out in the world the longest and still enjoyed sampling what was out there, whereas Gannon was just getting his feet wet. His mother would best grab him now before he discovered the true meaning of women.

"I'll make a deal with you, Mom," he decided to say, reaching out and gently squeezing her hand. "If I ever meet a woman who can hold my interest, you'll be the first to know."

* * *

Brittany sank into the chair opposite the man's desk. Luther Banyon was the attorney who'd sent her the recent letter, advising her that Gloria McIntyre, the woman who'd sent her that handwritten letter over six months ago, had died of ovarian cancer at the age of forty-four. That meant Gloria had only been sixteen when she'd given birth to Brittany.

Her tongue pressed against her sealed lips as she thought about how unfair it was to lose the mother she'd only just found. The letter from Ms. McIntyre had answered a lot of questions Brittany had always had. She'd known she had been given up at birth. That had been evident from her trek from foster home to foster home during her adolescent years.

There had been a time in her teens when she'd desired to find her birth mother, but after a while she'd gotten over it and had accepted things as they were. She'd moved on with her life, finishing high school at the top of her class and going on to college, then taking out a loan and opening Etiquette Matters.

"Now, Ms. Thrasher, we can begin."

Mr. Banyon pulled her out of her reverie. She had arrived in Phoenix a couple of hours ago, picked up a rental car and had come to his office straight from the airport.

"As stated in my letter, Gloria McIntyre died last month. I hadn't known she'd hired a private investigator to locate you until after she'd passed. That explains some things."

Brittany raised a brow. "What does it explain?"

"What she's been doing with her money for the past five years. When she died, her savings account was down to barely anything. And her home, although it has been paid off for years, was almost in foreclosure due to back taxes."

The man paused and said, "The doctor gave her five years to live and she used every day of those five years trying to find you. I'm so sorry her time ran out before the two of you could meet. She was a fine woman."

Brittany nodded. "Were you her attorney for long?"

"For over twenty years. She was married to Hugh McIntyre, but he died close to eight years ago. They never had any children. I guess it was after Hugh died that she decided she wanted to find you, the child she'd given away at sixteen."

Brittany didn't say anything. And then, "Mr. Banyon, your correspondence said she left a sealed letter for me."

"Yes, and she also left something else."

"What?"

"Her home. Though I must tell you that although it's been willed to you, there's a tax lien on it and it's due to be auctioned off tomorrow."

Brittany's chest tightened. "Tomorrow?"

"Yes. So if you want your mother's home, you arrived in the nick of time."

Brittany nodded. Yes, she wanted her mother's home because it was the key to who her mother was and why and how she'd made the decision that she had over twenty-eight years ago.

"And the items in the house?"

"Everything is still intact. However, house and contents are due to be auctioned. If someone else outbids you, you will have to negotiate with them and reach some sort of agreement or settlement as to the contents. All the city is concerned about is making sure the back taxes are recovered."

"I understand. Where will the auction take place tomorrow and what time?"

"I'll have my secretary provide you with all the information you need. Now if you will excuse me, I'll get that letter."

Brittany pulled in a deep breath at the same time she felt her heart soften. She'd known from the last letter that Gloria McIntyre wasn't one to say a lot, but what she did say had a profound impact. This letter was no different.

To my daughter, Brittany Thrasher, I leave my home and all my worldly goods and possessions. They aren't much, but they are mine to pass on to you with the love of a mother who always wanted the best for you.
Gloria McIntyre

"Are you all right, Ms. Thrasher?"

Brittany glanced up and met Mr. Banyon's concerned

gaze. "Yes, I'm fine. Do you know how much the back taxes amount to?"

"Yes, we're looking at almost five years' worth," he said, browsing through a stack of papers. "Here we are. It comes to close to seventy thousand dollars."

Brittany blinked. "Seventy thousand dollars!"

Mr. Banyon nodded. "Yes. Although the house itself isn't all that large, it sits on a whole lot of land and it has its own private road."

Brittany swallowed deeply. Seventy thousand dollars was more than she'd expected to part with. But it really didn't matter. She'd manage it. The business had had a good year. Paying the back taxes to gain possession of her mother's house was something she had to do. Something she wanted to do.

Her mother.

The thought made her quiver inside. Her only regret was that they'd never met. She could only fantasize about the type of relationship they would have shared if there had been more time. Just the thought that the reason the taxes had gotten delinquent in the first place was because her mother had placed locating her as her top priority was almost overwhelming.

"Is there a way I can get inside the house?" she asked Mr. Banyon.

He shook his head. "Unfortunately, there is not. It's locked and the keys have become the property of the city of Phoenix. They will be given to whoever becomes the new owner tomorrow. Ms. McIntyre's home is a rather nice one, but I can't and won't try to speculate as to who else might be interested."

Nodding, she stood. "Well, I intend to do everything in my power to make sure I become the new owner tomorrow."

"I know that's what Ms. McIntyre would have wanted and I wish you the best."

A few moments later after leaving Mr. Banyon's office, Brittany punched Gloria McIntyre's address into the car's GPS system. The directions took her a few miles from the Phoenix city limits, to a beautiful area of sprawling valleys.

She turned off the main highway and entered a two-lane road lined by desert plants. When the GPS directed her down a long private road, she slowed her speed to take in the beauty of the area covered in sand and tumbleweeds. Although this was the first week of December, the sun was shining bright in the sky. When the private road rounded a curve at the end of the drive, she saw the house with a wrought-iron fence around its ten acres of land. With all the cacti and a backdrop of a valley almost in the backyard, the scene looked like a home on the range.

She stopped the car and a feeling of both joy and pain tightened her chest. This was the house her mother had lived in for over twenty years and was the house she had left to her.

Mr. Banyon was right. It was modestly sized but it sat on a lot of land. The windows were boarded up; otherwise, she would have been tempted to take a peek inside. Several large trees in the front yard provided shade.

Something about the house called out to her, mainly because she knew it was a gift from a woman whom she'd never met but with whom she had a connection nonetheless. A biological connection.

As she put her car in gear to drive away, she knew whatever it took, when she left the auction tomorrow, this house would be hers.

Chapter 3

Galen had never been one not to take advantage of golden opportunities. Plus, he'd discovered a fascination with the auction mart since the day he'd bid on his first old muscle car. Snagging another one cheap was what drew him to the newest Phoenix auction today.

In addition to the car auction going on, there were several other things up on the auction block. Foreclosed homes, jewelry, electronic equipment, music memorabilia and trading cards. None of those items interested him. All he wanted was that classic 1969 Chevelle he'd heard about. After which, he would return home and continue to work on Sniper, the video game SID planned to unveil at the Video Game Expo in Atlanta in the spring.

Right now the biggest thing on his, Eric and Wesley's minds was the success of Turbine Force, the game they had debuted earlier that year. Because of an extremely good marketing campaign—thanks to his brother Jonas's firm—at present Turbine Force was the number-one-selling video game this holiday season.

He slowed his pace when his cell phone went off and pulled it out of his back pocket. "Yes?"

"Where are you?"

Galen rolled his eyes. "If I wanted you to keep up with me, Eli, I would be tweeting on Twitter."

"Funny. So where are you?"

Galen glanced at his watch. The auction for the Chevelle was starting in twenty minutes and he needed to be in place. "I'm at the auction mart. That Chevelle I was telling you about goes on the block today. What's up?"

He engaged in all-about-nothing chitchat with his brother for all of five minutes. Eli was the attorney in the family and handled SID's business concerns.

After putting away his cell phone, Galen headed toward the auction area. Adrenaline rushed through his veins. There was no telling how many car enthusiasts would be there waiting to buy and—

"Brittany Thrasher! I can't believe it!"

"Nikki Cartwright! I can't believe it, either."

Galen couldn't believe it, either, when the two women held their little reunion right in the middle of the floor and blocked the aisle. Anyone trying to maneuver around them had to squeeze by the huge decorated Christmas tree standing front and center.

He was about to follow the crowd and walk around

the two when something about one of the women caught his attention. He slowed his pace and stared. He knew the one in the business suit. She was the woman whose cab he'd hijacked in New York six months ago. He'd recognize her anywhere, although now she was smiling instead of frowning.

Hell, he'd had a mental snapshot of her since that day. There were some things a man couldn't forget and for him a gorgeous woman topped the list. At that moment a primitive instinct took hold of him and he drew in a deep breath, absorbed in the implication of what it meant. Whatever else, he was no fool. He knew the signs, fully understood the warning, but it was up to him if he wanted to heed them. Desire was a potent thing. Too much of it could get you into trouble.

He'd desired women before, hundreds of times. But there was something about this woman that was tempting him all the way to the bone.

He stepped out of the flow of the crowd and moved off to the side, feigning interest in the rack of brochures in front of him. As he pretended to read a brochure that listed over fifty Elvis items being auctioned, he listened to the women's conversation. Okay, eavesdropping was rude, but hadn't this same woman told him he needed to be taught manners?

He would consider it research. He wanted to know who she was and why was she here causing all sorts of crazy thoughts to go through his mind. He glanced over at her. She had tilted her head to the side while talking and he thought there was beauty in her neck, a gracefulness. And he liked the sound of her voice. Hell, he'd liked it that day in New York. He'd just been in too much of a rush to truly appreciate it at the time.

The last thing he wanted was to be seen, in case she remembered him, more specifically his lack of manners. And he knew firsthand that some women had long memories. They also were driven to get even. Galen wasn't up for that today. To be honest, he was distracted. He had a project in his garage that needed his absolute attention, so technically he had no business being here. But he had to bid on that '69 Chevelle.

The Chevelle.

He glanced at his watch and moaned. The bidding had already begun and more than likely the entry doors had been closed. He had missed out on the opportunity to own the car he'd always wanted because of his attention to this woman. Now he'd be forced to do an off-bid for the car, which meant if others were interested, the bidding war could go on forever. He pulled in a disgusted breath. They said payback was a bitch. Was losing out on that Chevelle his payback for the grief he'd caused the woman six months ago? He wasn't ready to accept his punishment.

He wasn't ready to do anything but find out who she was and why their paths had crossed yet again. Not that he was complaining. He listened more closely to their conversation to try to find out as much as he could about her.

There was a reason he was drawn to her. A reason why such a cool, calm and reserved sort of guy like himself would love to cross the floor, interrupt their conversation and pull her into his arms and kiss her. To be quite honest, he wanted to do more than just kiss her.

He figured he was going through some sort of hormonal meltdown. Over the years he'd learned to deal with an overabundance of testosterone. But he was definitely having trouble doing so today.

After finding out who she was, he might decide to come out of hiding and make a move. They were not in New York, squabbling over a cab. She was in Phoenix, the Steele neck of the woods, and for her that could be a good thing or a bad thing.

Brittany couldn't help but smile as she stared at Nikki. It had been over twelve years since they'd seen each other. At fourteen they had been the best of friends and had remained that way until right before their sixteenth birthdays when Nikki's father, who'd been in the navy, had received orders to move his family from the Tampa Bay area to San Diego.

They had tried staying in touch, but in Brittany's junior year of high school, when Mrs. Dugan got sick, Brittany had been sent to another foster home. During that first year with the Surratts, she had been too busy getting adjusted to her new family and new school to stay in contact.

"You look the same," she couldn't help but say to Nikki. She still had her curly black hair and her energetic chocolate-brown eyes. She truly hadn't aged at all.

"And so do you," Nikki replied on a laugh. "Are we really twenty-eight already?"

Brittany chuckled. "Afraid so. So what are you doing in Phoenix?"

"I live here now. After I graduated from high school in San Diego I followed a group of friends to the university here. I got a job with a photography firm after I graduated and I've been here since."

"How are your parents?"

"They're fine and still living in San Diego. Dad's retired now and driving Mom nuts. My brother Paul got married and has two kids, so the folks are happy about that."

Brittany nodded. "Well, I'm still single. What about you?"

"Heck, yes. I'm building a career in freelance photography and not a career of heartache due to men. And that's all the single guys in this city will give you. Now tell me about you, and please don't say you've been living in Phoenix all this time and our paths never crossed."

Brittany smiled. "No, I just arrived in town yesterday. In fact this is my first visit to Phoenix." And because Nikki had been her best friend during that phase of her life when she'd wanted to know her mother, she couldn't help but say in an excited voice, "And I'm here because of my mother."

Nikki's face lit up like a huge beam of light, and the smile and excitement made her face glow. "You found her?"

"No, actually she found me." Then sadness eased into Brittany's eyes when she added, "But we didn't get a chance to meet before she died."

"Oh, Brit," Nikki said, giving her a huge hug. "I'm sorry. What happened?"

Brittany found herself telling Nikki the entire story and why she was in Phoenix and there at the auction.

"Well, I believe things will work out for you. There are so many foreclosures out there, you might not have much competition in the bidding. I wish you luck because I know how much getting that house means to you. It's your only link to your mother."

Brittany nodded. "I'll do anything to get it. I already got my loan approval letter, so the money is not a problem. I just hope things go smoothly."

Nikki smiled. "And they will. I'll keep my fingers crossed. Now tell me, are you still living in Tampa? And what do you do there?"

"I'm still in Tampa and I own Etiquette Matters, a mobile etiquette school. I and the ten people I employ travel all over the country and hold seminars and teach classes. Each of us is assigned a certain section of the country. Things are going great because a number of corporations have begun introducing business etiquette and protocol as part of their corporate image training."

"Wow, that sounds wonderful. So when can we get together? There is so much that we need to catch up on," Nikki said.

"What about dinner later? If everything works

out—and I'm keeping positive that it will—I'll have reason to celebrate. And I plan on staying for a couple of weeks when I get the house. I want to move in and spend time there, knowing it was where my mother once lived."

Shivers of excitement raced up Brittany's spine when she added, "And what you said earlier is true. It is my one connection to my mother."

Galen waited until the women had exchanged contact information by way of business cards and hugged for what he hoped would be the last time before they finally headed in different directions.

The conversation between them had lasted a good twenty minutes. They had been so busy chatting away, catching up on old times as well as the new, that they hadn't even noticed him standing less than ten feet from them in the same spot, eavesdropping the entire time. It had been time well spent, because he'd gotten a lot of information about her.

Her name was Brittany Thrasher. She was twenty-eight, she lived in Tampa and she owned some sort of etiquette school that taught proper protocol and manners. He shook his head. Go figure.

He also knew all about the house she would be bidding on and why she wanted it so badly. It was a house on a private road off Rushing Street. He knew the area.

Galen glanced at his watch and figured he would hang around after all and make sure he and Brittany

Thrasher got reacquainted on more pleasant terms. It was time she saw that he wasn't such a bad guy. He'd just had an off day that time in New York. He would just throw on the Steele charm, talk her into taking him along when she went and took a tour of her new house. No telling where things would lead from there.

He was about to head in the direction she'd gone when another conversation caught his ears. This time between two men who were standing together talking.

"Are you sure the house off Rushing Street is going on the block today?" the short, stocky man asked his companion, a taller bald-headed guy.

"I'm positive. I verified it was listed in the program. If the rezoning of the area goes as planned—and I have no reason to believe that it won't with all the money we're pouring into the rezoning commissioner's election campaign—I figure that within a year, that property will be approved for commercial use."

The short, stocky man chuckled. "Good. Then we can tear the house down and use all that land to build another one of our hotels. We just need to make sure no one else outbids us for it."

Galen watched the men walk off. Evidently they wanted the same house Brittany would be bidding on. He shrugged, thinking it wasn't any of his business. That was the nature of an auction and there was no reason for him to get involved. Then he released a short laugh. Who in the hell was he fooling? Even when she had been in New York he'd made her his business. Time just hadn't lent itself for anything more than a confrontation between them.

He glanced at his watch before pulling his cell phone out of the back pocket of his jeans. The push of one button had his phone connected to Eli.

"What do you want, Galen?"

He smiled. Eli was the moody brother. Ready for chitchat one minute and a grouch the next. "I'm still here at the auction mart. I need you to fax me a loan approval letter with an open line of credit."

"What do you think I am, your banker?" his brother snapped.

"Just work miracles and do it and stop whining."

"Dammit, what's the fax number?"

"How the hell do I know? Just look it up." He quickly hung up the phone before Eli decided to get real ugly.

Galen made his way toward the auction area. Following the crowd, he wondered just when he'd begun rescuing damsels in distress. It was a disconcerting thought for a Steele, but in this case it was one he was looking forward to doing.

Chapter 4

Brittany got nervous as she glanced around the room. It was crowded, wall to wall. She knew there were fifteen homes being auctioned off today and she hoped none of these people were interested in the one she wanted. She would do as Nikki had suggested and think positive.

She smiled when she thought of how she'd run into her friend again after all these years. Although she'd had other friends, she'd never felt that special closeness with them that she'd felt with Nikki. And now they had agreed to do a better job of staying in touch and would start off rekindling their friendship by going out to dinner tonight. They had so much to catch up on.

She checked her watch. The auction would start in less than ten minutes and she was already nervous. This was the first time she'd ever attended an auction and hoped it wouldn't take long to get to her house.

Her house.

Already she was thinking of it as hers. She couldn't wait to go inside and look around. And she bet if she tried hard enough she would be able to feel her mother's presence. She shifted in her seat at the same time the hair on the back of her neck stood up. She scanned the room, wondering about the reason for her eerie feeling. But she didn't know anyone in the room, and no one here knew her.

The announcer at the front of the room hit his gavel on the table several times to get everyone's attention. She glanced down at the program and saw her house was listed as number eight. She pulled in a nervous breath when the auctioneer announced the auction had begun.

Galen was satisfied to sit in the back where he could see everything going on, and had a pretty good view of Brittany Thrasher. He also had a good view of those two guys who wanted her house. Of course he didn't plan to let them have it. Hopefully she had enough cash on hand to handle her own affairs, but in case she didn't, then unknowingly she had a guardian angel.

The thought of him being any woman's angel had him chuckling. He didn't do anything without an ulterior motive, and in her case he didn't have to dig deep to find out what it was. He wanted her in his bed. Or, if she preferred, her bed. It really didn't matter to him at this point.

He leaned back in his chair as he thought about all the heat the two of them could and would generate. But he had a feeling that with Brittany Thrasher he would need to proceed with caution. There was something about her and this intense desire he was feeling whenever he looked at her that he just couldn't put his finger on. But he would.

"Now we will move on to house number eight," the auctioneer was saying, interrupting his thoughts. For now it was a good thing.

"Who would like to open the bid?"

Brittany's heart raced when the bidding had officially begun on her house. She had gone on the Internet last night and visited the Web site that outlined the most effective way to participate in an auction. Rule number one said you should not start off the bid. Instead you should scope out the bidders to see if and when you could enter the fray. The key was knowing how much money you had and working with that.

The minimum bid had been set and so far the bidding remained in what she considered a healthy range with only three people actually showing interest. The highest bid was now at thirty-five thousand with only two people left bidding. She decided to enter at forty-six thousand.

She kept her eyes straight ahead on the auctioneer and didn't bother looking back to see who the other bidders were. That was another rule. Keep your eyes on the prize and not your opponents.

"We have a bid of fifty-two thousand. Do I hear fifty-three?"

She lifted her hand. "Fifty-three."

"We have a fifty-three. What about fifty-five?"

"Fifty-five."

Brittany couldn't resist looking sideways and saw a short, stocky man had made the bid. A nervousness settled in the pit of her stomach at the thought that the man wanted *her* house.

"We've got fifty-five. Do I hear fifty-seven?"

She lifted her hand. "Fifty-seven."

"The lady's bid is fifty-seven. Do I hear a sixty?"

"Seventy."

Brittany gasped under her breath at the high jump. Her approval letter was for a hundred thousand. She'd figured since the taxes were less than that it would be sufficient. Now she practically squirmed in her seat.

"We have seventy. Do I hear a seventy-two?"

She raised her hand. "Seventy-two." There were only two people left bidding, and she wondered how far the man would go in his bids.

She couldn't help but turn at that moment and regard the man. He flashed a smile that didn't quite reach his eyes. He wanted her house and—

"We have seventy-two. Can we get a seventy-five?" the auctioneer interrupted her thoughts by asking.

"Seventy-five," the man quickly spoke up.

The room got silent and she knew why. They had

reached the amount of the taxes that were due, but the auctioneer would continue until someone had placed the highest bid.

"We have seventy-five. Can we get eighty?"

Galen sighed, getting bored. The bidding for this particular house could go on all evening and he was ready for it to come to an end. It was obvious to everyone in the room that both of the two lone bidders wanted the house and would continue until someone conceded. He seriously doubted either would.

"We have eighty-six. Can we get an eighty-eight?" the auctioneer asked.

The short, stocky man raised his hand at eighty-eight.

"Can we get ninety?"

Brittany raised her hand. "Ninety." She had sent a text message to her banker for an updated approval letter asking for an increase but hadn't gotten a response. What if he was out of the office and hadn't gotten her request? She couldn't let anyone else get her house.

She glanced across the room at the man bidding against her. He appeared as determined as she was to keep bidding.

"We have ninety. Can we get ninety-two?"

"Two hundred thousand dollars."

Everyone in the room, including Brittany and the short, stocky man gasped. Even the auctioneer seemed surprised. Brittany closed her eyes feeling her only connection to her mother slipping away and a part of her couldn't believe it was happening.

"We have a bid of two hundred thousand dollars from the man in the back. Do we have two-ten?" No one said anything. Both Brittany and the short, stocky man were still speechless.

"Going once, going twice. Sold! The house has been sold to the man in the rear. And I suggest we all take a fifteen-minute break."

The people around her started getting up, but Brittany just sat there. She couldn't believe what had just happened. She had lost her mother's house. Her house.

She glanced over at the short, stocky man and he seemed just as disappointed as she felt. He nodded in her direction before he and the man he was with got up and walked out. The room was practically empty now with everyone taking advantage of the break. There was nothing left for her to do but leave. However, she couldn't help wondering the identity of the individual who had won her house. She really needed to get that person's name and if nothing else, hopefully she could negotiate with him to purchase her mother's belongings and—

"Fancy running into you again."

With so much weighing heavily on her mind, it took Brittany some effort to lift her head up to see who was talking to her. As soon as her gaze collided with the man's green eyes, she knew. Her mouth gaped open as she stared at him while he stood there smiling down at her.

"Wh-where did you come from?" she stuttered as she tried recovering from shock.

This was the same man who, even with all his less-than-desirable manners, had been able to creep into her dreams once or twice. She swallowed knowing it had been more often than that. And just thinking about those times sent a shiver through her. Fantasizing about him in her dreams was one thing, but actually seeing him again in the flesh was another.

What was he doing in Phoenix, and better yet, why did their paths have to cross again? Especially now?

"Where did I come from?" he asked, repeating her question as if he'd found it amusing. "I came from my house this morning and don't worry I came by car and not by cab."

She glared at him. If he thought that line was amusing he was wrong. All it did was remind her of just how impolite he'd been that day. That's really what she should be remembering, not thinking about the way the smile touched his lips, or what a gorgeous pair of eyes he had, or why even now when she had just lost the one thing she'd ever wanted in life, that she could feel the charge in the air between them. The heat. She'd felt it that day in New York, too, even with all her anger.

She hadn't taken the time to analyze it until a few days later, in the privacy of her bedroom when every time she would close her eyes she would see him looking so extremely handsome and dressed in a tux. And his pants had been unzipped. A sensation stirred in her belly at the memory.

Automatically, her gaze lowered to his zipper and she was grateful he was more together this time. Boy, was he. He was wearing a pair of jeans and a white Western shirt and a pair of scuffed boots. He was holding a dark brown Stetson in his hand, and she appreciated that at least he didn't have it on his head. Someone evidently hadn't told a couple of the men who'd attended the auction that it was bad manners to wear a hat inside a building.

And he was tall. She had to actually tilt her head back to look at him. He was built and she particularly liked the way his jeans stretched tight across his thighs. His shoulders were broad beneath his tailored shirt. She could tell.

The sight of him could make a woman drool, and as she continued to study him she remembered how his eyes had captured her from the first. Although she hadn't wanted them to. Those gorgeous Smokey Robinson eyes. She'd thought that then and was thinking the same thing now.

"Small world, isn't it?"

His statement made her realize she was still sitting down. The shock of losing her house hadn't worn off. She slowly stood up and didn't miss the way the green-eyed gaze traveled over her when she did so. She rolled her eyes. She was a big girl and could handle lust for what it was. He was a man and, she presumed, a single man. At least he wasn't wearing a ring, not that it meant anything these days. Besides, no matter how good he looked she couldn't forget that he was the epitome of rude.

And she was quick to size him up. He was a man on the prowl. She'd met more than one in her day and had always managed to convince them to prowl someplace else, in some other woman's neck of the woods. She'd discovered long ago that the whole idea of sex was overrated. She certainly hadn't gotten anything out of it so far.

"So, what about you? Where did you come from?" he prompted.

She thought that perhaps they were standing too close. Had he taken a step closer and she hadn't noticed it? She glanced around. The room was completely empty except for them.

"Doesn't matter where I'm from because I'm on my way back there." She glanced at her watch. "If you will excuse me, I need to find someone."

"Who?"

She tightened her lips to keep from saying it wasn't any of his business but decided not to. Besides, if he had been in the room during the bidding, there was a chance he might know the identity of the person who'd won her house.

"The man who placed the winning bid on the house I wanted. I really need to see him," she said.

"Okay."

When he didn't step back she moved around him.

"Have a nice day," she said, throwing the words over her shoulder as she headed for the exit door.

"Where are you going? We haven't been introduced."

She stopped and turned to him. She refused to be rude even if he had a history of doing so. "I'm rather in a hurry. Like I said, I've got to find—"

"Me."

Brittany tilted her head slightly. "Excuse me?"

A slow, sinfully sensual smile touched his lips. "I said in that case you're looking for me. I'm Galen Steele and I'm the person who placed the winning bid on house number eight."

Brittany took a step back thinking that couldn't be possible. This man, this rude man, could not be the new owner of *her* house. Not a man on the prowl. The man whose high testosterone level spoke volumes, to the point where even she—a person who'd never enjoyed sex—could read it. She guessed you didn't have to enjoy the act to feel the effect. Case in point, the way her heart was thumping in her chest.

"You have *my* house?" she asked, taking a deep, steadying breath. She still didn't want to believe such a thing was possible.

He nodded. "Signed, sealed and delivered. But it could be yours. I'm definitely willing to negotiate, Ms....?"

"Thrasher. Brittany Thrasher." She brushed her fingers against her throat trying to keep up with him.

"Are you saying that you might want to part with the house?"

He shrugged. "Why not? It serves me no purpose. I already have a house that I happen to like."

She threw up her hands in frustration, anger and total confusion. "Then why did you bid on it?"

He chuckled. "Because I saw how much you wanted it and I figured it would be a good bargaining tool."

Her brows furrowed in confusion. "A bargaining tool for what?"

"For when we make a deal. I'm going to make an offer that I hope you can't refuse."

She pulled in a deep breath. Did he think she wanted the house that bad that he could make a quick profit right here and now? Evidently that's just what he thought. And unfortunately, he was right. She wanted that house.

"How much?" she decided to cut to the chase and ask.

He lifted a brow. "How much?"

"Yes, how much do you want for it?"

"A week."

"Excuse me? I must have misunderstood you."

He smiled. "No, you didn't. I won't take money for the house, Ms. Thrasher, but I will take a week. Just one week of your time, on my terms, and the house is yours, free and clear."

For a stretch of more than a minute, the only sound in the room was their breathing, and then Brittany spoke and she tilted her head back and her gaze locked with his as she stared up at him. "Let me get this straight.

You will turn over that house to me if I spend a week with you?"

He nodded slowly and the gaze holding hers didn't flinch or waver. It was steadfast and unmovable. "Yes, but on my terms, which includes living under my roof."

Galen watched as she crossed her arms over her chest, just like she'd done that day in New York, reminding him what a nice pair of breasts they were. Standing this close to her again was calling his attention to a number of things about her that he'd missed that day. Like how her bottom lip would start quivering when she was angry or how her eyes would darken from a caramel to a deep, rich chocolate when things weren't going her way. He wondered if that same transformation took place while she was in the bedroom making love.

Her eyes narrowed on him. "Mr. Steele, you've lost your mind. What you're proposing is preposterous."

"No, it's not. It's what I want and personally, I think it's a rather good deal considering what you'll be getting," he pointed out. "In the end you'll get what you want and I'll get what I want."

Fire leaped into her face and he actually got aroused watching it. He wondered if anyone ever told her how hot she looked when she was angry. "How can you even suggest such a thing? A decent man would never talk that way to a lady. How dare you."

He chuckled again. "Yes, how dare me."

"And why in the world would I want to live with you for a week? Give me one good reason."

He shrugged. "I'll do better than that. I'll give you two. First, you want that house, so that should be incentive enough. Because it's not, there's the issue of what you said that day in New York about someone teaching me some manners."

"Well, they should!"

"Then do it. I dare you. I dare you to stay with me for a week and teach me manners." He reached into his back pocket and pulled out his wallet. And then he handed her his business card.

"You have only forty-eight hours to make your decision to contact me. If I don't hear from you, then I will donate the house, the land and all its contents to charity. Goodbye, Ms. Thrasher."

Then he walked off and didn't look back.

Chapter 5

The maitre d' greeted Brittany with a smile. "Good evening and welcome to Malone's. May I help you?"

"Yes. I have dinner reservations with Nikki Cartwright."

"Ms. Cartwright has already been seated. Please follow me."

Brittany glanced around while the man led the way. Nikki had suggested that they meet here and Brittany was glad Nikki had when the man stopped at a table next to a window providing a majestic view of the Sonoran foothills.

Nikki beamed when she saw her and stood and gave her a hug. "Well, did you get your house?" she asked excitedly.

Brittany fought to hold back the tears that had been

threatening to fall since she'd left the auction mart. "No, I was outbid," she said as she took her seat.

"Oh, Brit, I'm so sorry. I know how much getting that house meant to you. Have you talked to the new owner to see if you can at least get your mother's belongings because the house was willed to you?"

Brittany shook her head in disgust. "The man and I talked about a lot of things, but we never got around to that. He was so busy telling me how I'd be able to get the house from him free and clear."

"Really? How?"

"I have to live with him for a week."

Nikki nearly choked as she sipped on her water. "What?"

"You heard me right. He offered to sign the house over to me if I'd agree to spend a week with him."

Nikki looked aghast. "Just who is this guy? Of all the nerve."

"His name is Galen Steele and I have—"

"Galen Steele?" Nikki sat straight up in her chair. "Are you sure?"

"Yes, I'm sure. He gave me his business card and I have forty-eight hours to get back to him with my decision."

Nikki shook her head. "I can't believe he actually approached you like that, a complete stranger."

"We're not exactly strangers," Brittany said and then went on to explain how they'd met over the cab. "Luckily, I was early for the airport and another cab was dispatched within minutes. But still, before he left I told him that someone should teach him some manners. So now he wants me to move in with him and do just that."

"To teach him manners?" Nikki asked.

Brittany gave her friend a straight look. "I wasn't born yesterday, Nikki. I'm sure a class on manners isn't all he's expecting."

Nikki nodded. "Knowing those Steeles, it's probably not."

She raised a brow. "Do you know him?"

"Not personally, but there aren't many single women in Phoenix who don't know of the Steeles. There are six of them. All handsome as sin with green eyes that can make your panties wet if they look at you long enough. The green eyes are from their mother's side of the family. She used to be a fashion model and was well-known in her day. I heard that even now she's still quite beautiful."

"And Galen has five brothers?"

"Yes, and all of them were born within a year of each other. Galen is the oldest. It seems their father was serious about keeping his wife pregnant. And in addition to being handsome, all those Steeles are very successful. The only one I've ever said more than two words to is Jonas. He owns a marketing firm and I've done freelance photography work for him once or twice. Jonas is a pretty nice guy, but all those Steeles have one thing in common besides good looks, success and green eyes."

"What?" Brittany wanted to know.

"They are hard-core womanizers, all six of them, which is why women consider them the 'Bad News Steeles.' People claim they got their womanizing ways from their father. I heard he used to be something else before settling down and marrying Eden Tyson."

Nikki then leaned over the table. "With you owning an etiquette school, you'll be the perfect person to teach him manners. Are you going to take Galen Steele up on his offer?"

Brittany pushed a lock of hair out of her face. "Of course not! He doesn't even know what I do for a living."

Nikki chuckled. "There's a joke around town that a woman hasn't been bedded unless she's been bedded by a Steele. They're supposed to be just that good."

No man was that good, Brittany thought. At least none in her past had been worth the trouble. "Well, I plan on contacting him tomorrow. There has to be another way."

Nikki shrugged as a half smile eased across her lips. "I don't know. I understand when they see a woman they want, they go after her. Of course they drop her after a while, but there are a lot of women who would love to be in your shoes right now, including me. Not for Galen, mind you, but I've always had this thing for Jonas. He's a hottie."

Brittany stared across the table at her long-lost friend. "Let me get this straight. If given the chance you would accept his terms of an affair?"

"Of course," Nikki said without any thought. "I'm a

career woman and I've pretty much given up the notion of finding Mr. Right because it seems they're already taken. What you have out there now are men like the Steeles, the Hard-Ons, the Idiots and the Dawgs. They are the men who want one thing and one thing only. I'm prepared for them because personally, I want only one thing myself. I no longer have any grandiose ideas of settling down, marrying a man who is my soul mate, having babies and living happily ever after. All it takes is for me to watch divorce court on television to know it doesn't work that way. At least not anymore and not for most people."

Brittany felt sad for her friend. When they were teenagers, Nikki had dreamed of a knight in shining armor.

"What about you?" Nikki interrupted her thoughts by asking. "I remember you weren't in a rush to ever marry. You wanted to see the world first. And," she added, lowering her voice, "you were sort of against men because of what that man tried to do to you that time."

Nikki's words suddenly yanked Brittany out of the present and pushed her right smack back into the past when she'd been thirteen and Mr. Ponder, a male friend of one of her foster parents, had tried forcing himself on her. He would have succeeded had she not bit him hard enough for him to let her go. It was the first time she'd run away from a foster home. After telling the policemen who'd found her what happened—or almost happened—the authorities had placed her in another foster home right away.

That move had been a blessing because that's when she'd met Nikki. Nikki's family had lived across the street from the Dugans. At first the trauma of what the man had tried doing left Brittany withdrawn, confused and alone. But all that changed when Nikki became her friend. At some point she'd felt comfortable enough with Nikki to share her secret.

"Brit, maybe I shouldn't have brought it up," she heard Nikki saying. "I'm sorry."

She met her friend's apologetic gaze. "No, I'm fine, although I haven't thought of it in years. But now I'm wondering if that episode has anything to do with why..."

When her words faltered, Nikki raised a brow and asked, "Why what?"

Brittany glanced around to make sure no one was listening to their conversation, leaned over the table and whispered, "Why I don't enjoy sex like most women."

"It might and then again, it might not. Some men are just selfish in the bedroom. It's all about them and they could care less if you get your pleasures or not. You might have been involved with those types."

Nikki smiled and then continued. "What you need is a man who has the ability to tap into those hidden pleasures. And if that's true, based on what I've heard, a Steele is just the man who can do it. I know several women who had short-term affairs with them and their only regret was missing out on all that pleasure. They claim that when it comes to fulfilling a woman's fantasy, those 'Bad News Steeles' are top-notch.'"

Brittany waited while the waiter placed menus in front of them. When the man walked off, she said, "And what if I don't have any hidden pleasures for anyone to tap into?"

Nikki gave her a somber look. "If you don't enjoy sex at the hands of a Steele, then I would suggest you get some serious counseling. Although that pervert didn't succeed in doing anything, I can imagine it was a traumatic experience for you to go through at the time. You were only thirteen."

Yes, Brittany thought. She'd been only thirteen. Now she understood those looks Mr. Ponder used to give her and why she wasn't comfortable when she received those kind of looks now from men.

"Do you know what I think, Brit?"

Brittany glanced across the table at Nikki. It was hard to believe they hadn't seen each other in over twelve years. That special bond they'd always had seemed to just fall into place. Nikki had been there to help her through some rough times in her life and when Nikki had moved away, she had truly lost her best friend. There hadn't been anyone she could talk to, share her innermost fears and secrets with. She had felt truly alone.

"No, what do you think?" she asked.

"Of course it needs to be your decision, but in a way you can practically kill two birds with one stone. If you accept Galen Steele's offer, not only will you get your mother's house free and clear, but you'll also find out if your dislike of sex is something you need to explore professionally. But I have a feeling Galen Steele will unlock all the hidden pleasures locked away inside you. It takes a man with an experienced touch to do that, and I hear that's what Galen Steele has."

Brittany shook her head, not convinced the suggested approach was the right one. "I don't know, Nikki. The couple of guys I slept with before…I could only do it because I liked them, although I never fancied myself in love with them. I'm not sure I can have casual sex with anyone just for the sake of sex. Besides, I'm not all that certain I even like Galen Steele. Both times when our paths crossed he didn't impress me as someone with good manners."

Nikki threw her head back and laughed. "Manners are the last thing you'll think about when the big 'O' strikes. And trust me, Brit, you won't be doing it just for the sake of doing it. You'll be doing it for pleasure, and there's plenty of pleasure out there waiting for you. I think you just need the right man and I'm totally convinced Galen Steele is that man. Think about it."

Brittany nodded. She certainly had strong motivation for doing so—her house was at stake. However, like she'd told Nikki, she wasn't sure if she could engage in casual sex and enjoy it. Then again, she'd done it a couple of times with guys she was involved with at the time and hadn't enjoyed it, either.

She picked up her menu and eyed her friend over the top. "All right. I'll think about it."

* * *

Eli Steele glared at the man sitting on the opposite side of his desk. He'd often wondered about his oldest brother's mental state and this was one of those times. "Let me get this straight, Galen. You rushed me to fax that damn loan approval letter to you yesterday so that you could bid on some house you really don't want? A house you are now signing over to some woman you really don't know?"

Galen nodded slowly. "Yes, that sounds about right to me. You have a problem with any of it?" Eli was son number three and there was barely a two-year difference in their ages. It amused Galen how their father had kept their mother barefoot and pregnant for six years straight. She'd given birth to a son each year. They'd grown up close, and they still were, but that didn't mean they wouldn't rattle each other's cages at times. He often wondered how his mother had handled living in a house filled with so much testosterone.

"No, I don't have a problem with it because it's your money," Eli said.

"And you're my attorney," he reminded him, which his brother seemed to forget sometimes. In addition to being the corporate attorney for SID, Eli was legal counsel for several other private companies and was doing quite well for himself. Which was probably why a couple of years ago, right before his thirtieth birthday, he'd bought the perfect building for his law practice in downtown Phoenix: the hub of business activities, and right in the heart of the valley. Prime real estate property if ever there was any.

Galen would be the first to admit the high-rise building was a beautiful piece of architecture and had been a wise investment for his brother to make. It was huge, spacious and upscale. Eli's firm took up the entire twentieth floor. The other floors were leased, which brought him in a nice profit each month. Another plus was the view from Eli's office window. He saw straight into a penthouse fitness center across the street, and Galen could just imagine his brother sitting behind his desk checking out the women.

"I'll have the papers ready for you to pick up later this evening," Eli told him.

"Go ahead and overnight the deeds to her because I won't be seeing her again."

He decided not to tell Eli about the outlandish proposition he'd made to the woman, probably because knowing Eli, he wouldn't consider it outlandish at all. And under normal circumstances, neither would he. But again, he knew how much that house meant to Brittany Thrasher so for once he'd given in to his soft spot and not his hard-on.

He smiled thinking there were women who wouldn't believe he had a soft spot, and very few could touch it like Brittany Thrasher had.

Chances were she was on her way back home to Florida. He'd have loved to be there to see her face when she received the papers giving her the house, property and land, free and clear.

"Do you have her address?"

Galen rolled his eyes. "Why would I have her address? I met her only twice."

"Yet you're giving her a property worth a lot of money?"

Leave it to Eli to try and make things difficult. His brother had a habit of rationalizing things too much. "No, the house was already hers. I've already explained that it was willed to her by her biological mother."

"Gotcha. You're such a nice guy, a real champion of good causes," Eli said sarcastically. And then he added, "It's hard to believe there won't be anything in this for you."

It was hard for Galen to believe that, too. He'd made her that outlandish proposal, but hadn't really expected her to go for it. Not with her being Miss Manners and all. She probably figured his offer was just another display of his ill-mannered and brutish side. But he couldn't help but wonder how things might have been if she had accepted his offer.

He could just imagine spending a week behind closed doors with her. She would teach him manners and he would teach her how to let her hair down, live for the moment. He would love to see those caramel-colored eyes turn chocolate-brown from something other than anger. A full-blown orgasm would do the trick.

"Is there anything else? You're just sitting here not saying anything."

Eli's words whipped Galen's mind back on track and he quickly stood. "No, that's about it. If possible I'd like the papers sent today, so she'll get them tomorrow. She might want to return to Phoenix and go through her mother's belongings."

A part of him was counting on her doing so and he intended to make it his business to be around when she did. Maybe all wasn't lost after all.

"Excuse me, Galen, but I have work to do. Now you're just standing there, staring into space and smiling."

Galen shook his head. To know Eli was to love him. He could be such a pain in the ass. "You're going to the folks' for dinner tomorrow night?" he decided to ask before he left.

"Of course. Who could be brave enough to miss it? If we don't show up for Mom's Thursday-night family dinner hour, there's no telling what will happen the next day. She might decide to come around snooping."

Galen knew that to be true. Mercury hadn't shown up one night last month and before he could wake up Friday morning, Eden Steele was on his doorstep. She'd told him that because son number five had missed such an important family activity, she was duty-bound to spend the whole day with him. Unfortunately, Mercury hadn't been alone when their mother had shown up. By the end of the day, after driving their mother around town—to do some mother-and-son bonding as she'd called it—Mercury hadn't been too happy.

"Then I will see you tomorrow night." He turned to leave and then stopped and said, "And by the way, I like your new administrative assistant. She has nice legs."

Eli grunted. "I wouldn't know. I haven't noticed."

Liar, Galen thought. He happened to know Eli was a leg man. Chances were he'd not only noticed, but he'd already been between those same legs. If he hadn't gotten that far already, there was no doubt in Galen's mind that Eli was finalizing his plans to get there.

Galen couldn't help chuckling as he walked out the door. He wasn't mad at Eli. That was the Steeles' way. And why did another part of him wish things had worked out differently between him and Brittany Thrasher? It would have been nice had she agreed to his proposal. Just as well that she hadn't, though, because he had plenty of work to do back at his garage. He needed to get his mind back on track and finish working on his latest video game project.

But when it came to a woman who looked like Brittany Thrasher, he would trade in a bunch of electronic parts for her real body parts any day.

Brittany sat staring at her cell phone and the business card she had placed beside it. She had a decision to make and doing so wasn't easy. She had enjoyed dinner with Nikki; it'd been like old times as they'd reminisced and caught up on each other's lives. They had agreed to do lunch before Brittany returned home...if she didn't take Galen Steele up on his offer.

Drawing in a deep breath, she reached for her phone and then quickly snatched her hand back. She was not ready to do anything just yet. She glanced over at the clock. Only sixteen hours had passed since Galen Steele had made his offer and he'd given her forty-eight.

That meant she had thirty-two hours to go. Because she hadn't been sure what to expect with this trip to Phoenix, especially how long she would have to stay, she had purchased a one-way ticket. One of her employees was covering her etiquette training classes for the next couple of weeks, so she didn't have to worry about work, either.

She stood and decided that no matter how much she wanted her mother's home and the belongings inside it, she would not make any hasty decisions where Galen Steele was concerned. It was quite obvious the man wanted only one thing from her and it had nothing to do with teaching him manners like he claimed. Mind you, his manners could use some improving, but she wasn't that gullible to believe he wanted her to stay under his roof for seven days to perfect his pleases and thank-yous.

She lay across the bed and grabbed the remote to flick on the television. She was not a television person, but for lack of anything else to do for now, she would see if there was anything on the tube worth watching. She had thought of driving back out to her mother's house, but there would be no purpose served in doing that.

As she lay there looking at the television without actually seeing it, she couldn't help wondering about the pros and cons of staying with Galen for a week. He didn't come across as the type of man who would try and force a woman to do anything she didn't want to do. But still…

Would she have a guest bedroom, or did he assume

she would be sharing his? And just what type of manners did he want to be taught? Most people knew the basic manners; they just didn't use them. And then there was the issue of her little problem... If she spent an entire week with him, would Galen cure her of her sexual hang-ups? Her low libido had never bothered her. Now she was beginning to wonder if it should have.

She pulled the pillow from under her head and then smothered her face with it. It swallowed up her groan. This was all Galen's fault. The man not only had her thinking, but he also had her feeling things she'd never felt before. Nikki would think that was a good sign.

She removed the pillow off her face, tossed it aside and stared up at the ceiling. She thought about the last serious relationship she'd been involved in with Gilford Turner. For an entire year he would arrive after church on Sunday like clockwork and stay until Tuesday. They never discussed marriage and that had been fine with her as much as it had been with him. His mother had been the only one bothered by their lack of motivation to get to the altar. For them, there had been no big rush.

She hadn't fooled herself into thinking that she was in love with him or vice versa. They liked each other and that was as far as it went. That's why when he'd dropped by one day during the week to announce he wouldn't be coming back, with a smile on her face she'd gathered up all of his belongings, placed them in a box and walked him to the door and wished him well. In the days, weeks and months that followed, she hadn't pined after him, nor had she missed his presence. She had carried on with her life and her Sundays through Tuesdays had once again become her own.

And as for the sex…

She could honestly say she hadn't missed any of it because there hadn't been anything inspiring about it.

A year after Gilford, she'd tried getting back into the dating thing again and it took less than a month to decide she hadn't wanted the hassles, the aggravation or the drama of getting to know another man. Most tried to be slick and only had one thing on their mind. Sex. At some point she realized she'd rather have a root canal than to contemplate having sex with a man.

Would Galen be different? She was attracted to him, that much was a given. And around him she'd felt a sexual interest that she hadn't felt toward a man before, which could be considered a plus. And for the first time in her life she could admit to dreaming about hot, sweaty sex. Galen himself had crept into her dreams during those times.

Indulging her nervous habit, she bit her bottom lip. She had decisions to make and for now she needed her full concentration. She turned off the TV. She had to think. Boy, did she have to think.

Chapter 6

His cell phone rang and Galen absently pressed the Bluetooth in his ear without taking his gaze off the sixty pieces of software components in front of him. It was the middle of the day and he was in his air-conditioned six-car garage working on what would be the brain of his next video game. He had worked on what he considered the senses last night.

"This is Galen."

"Mr. Steele, this is Brittany Thrasher."

He shifted his gaze to a copy of the FedEx receipt Eli had dropped off earlier. Because he'd been busy at the time, he had placed it on his desk. He wasn't surprised she was calling. Evidently she'd gotten the overnight package and was calling to thank him.

"Yes, Ms. Thrasher?"

"I was wondering if we could meet somewhere and talk."

He lifted a brow, surprised. "You're still in Phoenix?"

"Yes."

He put down the pliers he'd been holding. If she was still in Phoenix that meant she was unaware he'd signed the house over to her. "And what do you want to talk about?"

"Your proposal. I have some questions about it."

He drew in a deep, steadying breath as he tried to get his heart rate under control, while at the same time ignore the throbbing in his groin. Was she seriously contemplating taking him up on his offer? He definitely hadn't expected her to do so. The decent thing to do would be to come clean and tell her that he'd signed the house over to her, so there was no need for them to discuss the proposal. But he couldn't help being curious about her questions.

"What kind of questions?" he heard himself asking.

"First of all, I want to know where I'll be sleeping while I'm under your roof."

Several visual images flashed through his mind. Maybe now was not a good time to tell her that if he had his way, she wouldn't be doing much sleeping. "Where would you want to sleep?" he decided to ask her.

"In a guest bedroom."

He smiled, not surprised. "That could be arranged for the first couple of days." There was no reason to tell her that if that's where she slept, then that's where he would also be sleeping.

"And I know granting this request might be a little difficult, especially for a man I'm teaching manners to, but I'd like you to promise to keep your hands to yourself."

He couldn't help but throw his head back and laugh. "When?"

"Excuse me?"

Oh, he wouldn't excuse her, not even a little bit. "I asked when am I supposed to keep my hands to myself?"

"At all times."

His smile widened. He hadn't done that since grade school when Cindy Miller had squealed to the teacher on him for kissing her neck. "Sorry, I can't make you that promise because I *do* intend to touch you," he said, deciding he might as well tell her the truth.

"Mr. Steele, this is only a coincidence but believe it or not, I teach manners for a living."

He chuckled. "You don't say."

"I do say. I own Etiquette Matters and I take my work seriously. If I decided to accept your proposal—and that's a big 'if'—my sole purpose would be to teach you manners."

"In that case, Ms. Thrasher, maybe the first thing on your list should be to teach me how to keep my hands off you." He leaned back in his chair, clearly enjoying this. He could imagine she was pretty damn annoyed with him about now.

"Is there any way we can renegotiate your offer?"

She had to be kidding. "No. I have something you want and you have something I want. You either come to live with me for a week or the house and its contents go to charity."

"You are being difficult, Mr. Steele."

He smiled. Now that she had surprised the hell out of him by showing an interest, she hadn't seen anything yet. "There's no reason for me to make it easy for you, Ms. Thrasher. I gave you my terms. You can either accept them or reject them. You have less than ten hours to decide."

He wished they were talking face-to-face. He figured her bottom lip was quivering in anger about now, and he would love to see, even better, he'd love to taste that anger.

"I'd like to make a counteroffer."

He shook his head. She didn't know when to give up. She was definitely persistent and he liked that about her because he was the same way. He didn't say anything for a while, deciding to let her statement hover between them for a minute. And then, "Because I consider myself a fair man, I'll let you do that. But we need to meet in person," he said. He rubbed his chin. "I can come to your hotel."

"I prefer we meet someplace else."

"If you insist. Let's meet at Regis. It's a coffee shop in downtown Phoenix, walking distance from your hotel."

"I never told you the name of my hotel."

He thought quick on his feet. "I didn't say that you did. I assume you're staying at one of the hotels downtown."

Not wanting to give her time to think about his slipup, he asked, "Are you not staying at a hotel downtown?"

She hesitated a quick minute before saying, "Yes, I am."

"Fine. I'll meet you at Regis in an hour. Goodbye." He then quickly ended the call before she could rethink it.

Brittany thought it was a beautiful day for walking. Besides, it gave her some extra time to think before actually meeting with Galen. Even though it was lunchtime and the sidewalk was crowded with people, she couldn't help being fascinated with downtown Phoenix.

Earlier that day she had gone on a tour of the state capitol and had checked out the Phoenix Art Museum. She had arrived in time to see a small play on the history of the state; however, she'd been so preoccupied with her thoughts that she hadn't really paid attention.

When she saw the sign for Regis up ahead, she began nibbling on her lips. Meeting with Galen Steele wouldn't be so bad if he wasn't so darn handsome. Her attraction to him had taken her by surprise, because no man ever captured her interest the way he had.

Annoyance seethed through her when she remembered that he was a man with only one thing on his agenda. It would be up to her to try and sway his mind about a few things. If he didn't go along with what she was going to suggest, what did she have to lose?

Her house, for starters.

That realization made her heart sink as she opened the door to the café. She only had to scan the place a few seconds before her gaze locked with his. In an instant she was drawn to the most captivating pair of green eyes anyone could possess. They would be her downfall if she wasn't careful. But how could a woman be careful around the likes of Galen? Just seeing him issued an invitation to take every risk and then some.

He stood when he saw her and she was impressed that he could display some manners when he wanted to. Only thing was, now that he was standing, her gaze shifted from his eyes to encompass all of him. He was wearing a pullover shirt and a pair of khakis. His stance was sexy as sin.

The sunlight pouring through the windows struck him at an angle that projected brilliant rays on his skin, which was the color of mahogany. And if that wasn't bad enough, his shoulders looked broader in that particular shirt.

She continued to hold his gaze as she released the door to step inside. This meeting was utterly ridiculous, really. His proposal had been absurd. And the thought that she was here to negotiate anything was absolutely crazy. What she should do was turn right around, open the door and leave. But she couldn't do that. This man stood between her and the one thing she wanted more than anything. A connection to her mother. He was the key. To be even more specific, he *had* the key.

She broke eye contact with him long enough to note that the café was packed but somehow he'd grabbed a table. Sighing deeply and with a tight smile plastered on her face, she moved toward him.

There would be nothing proper or graceful about the way he would take her the first time, Galen decided as he watched Brittany stroll in his direction. It didn't have to be in a bed. Any spot in his house would suffice. And they didn't have to be lying down. Taking her against a wall would be fine. He should be downright mortified with the direction of his thoughts. Definitely ashamed. But he wasn't.

He kept his gaze trained on her. She walked with confidence, grace and style. And the look on her face was that of a woman on a mission. A mission not to change the world, just his mind.

His eyes scanned her. She was wearing a denim skirt that hit below the knee and a modest blouse. Who did modest and below the knee these days? he wondered. Still, he had to admit that both items of clothing looked rather nice on her. The skirt did an awesome job of showing her curves, and the blouse emphasized the firmness of the breasts pressing against it. And those legs he'd admired yesterday were still looking pretty damn good today. He could imagine those legs wrapped around him after he got between them.

Was that sweat he was beginning to feel on his brow?

No matter, the lustful thoughts running through his mind were exhilarating. Hot and potent at their best. But that was okay because at some point he intended to turn those thoughts into reality.

As she got closer he couldn't help noticing that she had a prissy look, too prim and proper. For some reason he felt that a bout of hot, heavy and sweaty sex would suit her. He wanted to see her perfectly done hair get mussed up a bit. He wanted to be the one to nibble on that bottom lip, and he wanted to be the one to make love to her without an ounce of finesse.

When she reached his table, she held out her hand to him. "Mr. Steele."

Such formality. She had to be kidding, he thought, just seconds before saying, "Ms. Thrasher." And then he took a step closer and lowered his mouth to hers.

Before Brittany could move, his mouth was there, dead center on hers. And when she parted her lips in shock, it gave him the opening he needed to slide his tongue inside her mouth.

For a split second she forgot how to breathe, especially when she felt Galen's tongue giving her mouth a quick sweep before he pulled back, ending the kiss. In less than a minute he had taken the term *short and sweet* to a whole other level.

A quick glance indicated a number of people had witnessed the kiss. She narrowed her gaze at him. "It is not good manners to kiss in a public place."

He smiled, evidently amused. "It's not?"

"No."

"Do you want to go outside and continue, then?"

"Of course not!"

"A pity," he said, pulling a chair out for her. He brushed his fingers on her arms while doing so and she shivered, wondering if the touch had been accidental or if he'd meant to do it. She glanced over at him and from the smile on his face she knew he'd meant to do it.

And this was the man who wanted her to stay under his roof for a week. If he was taking these kinds of liberties in public, she could just imagine what he'd do in private. There was something about him that made her unbalanced, shaky, and she had to wonder if she had completely lost her mind to even be here with him.

"People are staring at us," she said in a low voice.

He shrugged. "Let them stare. They probably think we're lovers who didn't get enough of each other last night. They're just jealous."

She wondered if he was always this quick with a comeback and if his mind continuously revolved around sex. If nothing else, she was picking up on some heated vibes just sitting across the table from him. She wondered if he felt them or if her senses were the only ones under siege.

"You wanted to make a counteroffer."

His words had cut into her thoughts and she looked into his green eyes. Good Lord, the man was handsome. "Yes, that's right," she said, almost stumbling over the words.

"Would you care for something to eat and drink before we get started on the negotiations?"

"Coffee, please." What she needed was something stronger, but coffee would have to do.

She watched him motion to the waitress who came over with the coffeepot in her hand and ready to pour. After the woman walked away, he gave Brittany a chance to add her sweetener and take a sip before asking, "So, what's your counteroffer?"

Brittany breathed in deeply, shifted in her seat and said, "That I teach you manners for a week but I live in the house."

Galen immediately knew what house she was referring to, but decided to ask anyway. "And which house is that?"

"The one you won at the auction two days ago."

"Why? Once you carry out the terms of my offer it will be yours in a week to do whatever you want with it, so what's the hurry?"

"If I told you I doubt you'd understand."

"Try me."

"I'd rather not."

Galen knew that even if she had shared her reason, he would not have changed his plans. "I prefer that you stay at my place. In fact, I insist on it. However, I'd give you the key to go there whenever you want when you have some free time."

Genuine surprise touched her eyes. "You would?"

"Yes."

He thought her smile perfection and it almost made

him feel like a heel for playing her this way, when all
he had to do was tell her that as of ten o'clock yesterday
morning, the house had become hers anyway. But for
some reason he couldn't do that. He'd never expected
her to consider such an outlandish offer and now that
she had, he couldn't back down.

She took another sip of her coffee and he took a sip of
his, wishing it was a sip of her instead. That quick taste
he'd gotten of her when they'd kissed wasn't enough,
especially because he knew there was more where that
had come from. Locking lips again with her was not
something he was willing to pass up. And then there was
her perfume. The scent was as luscious as she looked.

"So, are you ready to give me your answer?" he
asked, while trying not to sound overly eager.

She looked up at him. "No, not yet. I have to think
this through to the end."

He could only think of one reason why she was
drawing this out and the thought of it annoyed him.
"Why? Do you have a boyfriend back home?"

"Of course not! If I did, I wouldn't be here contemplating your offer. Just what kind of woman do you
think I am?"

One who put too much emphasis on manners, he
thought but didn't say. She wanted to teach him manners,
and he wanted to show her that there was a time and
a place for manners, and there was a time and a place
not for them. "I don't know. What kind of woman are
you?" he responded.

He wondered how long he was going to last, sitting

here engaging in idle chitchat with her when all he wanted to do was take her somewhere and feel her body pressed next to his and indulge once more in the taste of her mouth. He knew he needed to proceed with caution with her, but he was finding it hard to do so.

"I'm a woman who takes life seriously," she said, frowning over at him.

His gaze automatically went to her lower lip. Seeing it quiver sparked a low burn in his groin and had his erection pressing hard against his zipper. She was annoyed, angry and probably frustrated and her facial features were letting him know it and turning him on in the process. He figured now would not be a good time to ask when was the last time she'd gotten buck-naked and wild in the bedroom. He knew for a fact that that was a good way to release tension and stress.

"I'm a man who takes life seriously, as well," he said, and from the look on her face, he could tell she doubted his sincerity.

"So what kind of manners do you want me to teach you?" she inquired before taking another sip of her coffee.

"What kinds are there?"

She took another sip of her coffee. "There are the basic manners about not putting your elbows on the table and what fork to use while eating. Then there are the business manners, party and entertainment etiquette, gift-giving etiquette, and the—"

"What about bedroom etiquette?"

He watched her lips tighten and enjoyed seeing that,

too. Anything she did with her lips aroused him. He took a sip of his coffee and noted she hadn't responded to his question. Had he hit a sore spot with her or something? That possibility called for further investigation.

"Bedroom etiquette?" she finally asked.

A slow smile touched his lips. "Yes, you know, the dos and don'ts while a couple is in the bedroom making love. I'm curious as to what's proper and what's not. Surely there are some specific manners governing that sort of thing."

"I'm sure there are."

"But those are the manners that you don't teach?" he asked. He had her swimming in unfamiliar waters—and he was enjoying it. He was good at reading people and he could tell this topic of conversation had her somewhat flustered. Was she one of those women who thought a discussion of sex should only take place behind closed doors and not over coffee in a restaurant?

"Ms. Thrasher?" She had clamped her mouth shut and now he was forcing her to open it again.

"I've never done so before, Mr. Steele."

"Please call me Galen, and why not? Are you saying no one has ever approached you for such instruction?"

She held his gaze and lifted her chin. "That's exactly what I'm saying. You are the first."

Galen took another sip of his coffee. She was upset with him and her features showed it. In addition to the quivering of her bottom lip, her brows arched in a cute formation over her eyes and her nostrils seemed to flare. Why did seeing all of that make adrenaline flow through his veins? If that wasn't insane, he didn't know what was.

"In that case, I'd love to be your first student, Brittany. I can call you Brittany, can't I?"

"I prefer you not be my first anything, and yes, you can call me Brittany."

Brittany took another sip of her coffee. He had turned those green eyes on her and she felt trapped by them. If he was playing some sort of game with her, then he was winning. The man had her tied up in all kinds of knots.

"But I am your first in at least two things that I know of, Brittany. Has anyone ever hijacked a cab from you before me?"

"No."

"Has anyone ever made a proposition like the one I have?"

"No."

"Seems like we're on a roll. We might as well continue."

She much preferred they didn't. "Why would you want to learn bedroom etiquette?" she decided to ask, more out of curiosity than anything.

"I might decide to date a real lady one of these days, and I wouldn't want to run her off with my less-than-desirable behavior behind closed doors. Right now I like to keep things simple, and simple for me is delivering pleasure beyond measure. In a rather naughty and raunchy, hot and sweaty sort of way. The women I'm into now enjoy it, but I need to know how far I can go."

Naughty and raunchy? Hot and sweaty? She swallowed tightly at the thought of that description given to sex. "I really wouldn't know."

His mere words were causing more havoc to her body than Gilford's touch ever did. She actually felt a heated sensation between her thighs that made her cross her legs.

"If you want me to teach you manners, Galen, I prefer sticking with those areas I'm familiar with," she said in a clipped tone.

He leaned back in his chair thinking he so liked ruffling her feathers. "Okay. And when will you let me know if you plan to teach me any manners at all? When will I know for certain that you've accepted my proposal?"

She placed her coffee cup aside. "You've given me forty-eight hours. If you don't hear from me within that time frame, then you'll know my decision."

He nodded slowly. "And if I hear from you?"

"Then we can go from there." She stood. "Thanks for the coffee. Goodbye, Galen."

He stood, as well. "Goodbye, Brittany, and I'll look forward to your phone call."

She turned and walked away, and he continued to stand there and stare at her, appreciating the sway of her hips with every step she took.

An hour or so later Brittany was pacing her hotel room. Every time she slowed her pace and closed her eyes for a moment, she could see Galen Steele's arrogant smile in her mind.

Of all the nerve for him to ask her about bedroom manners. As far as she was concerned, there wasn't such a thing. What a couple did behind closed doors was acceptable as long as they both agreed and were comfortable with it, even if it meant swinging butt-naked from a chandelier. Of course he'd only asked to rattle her, she was sure of it, and it didn't help matters that she didn't have a clue as to what he was talking about. She wouldn't know naughty and raunchy or hot and sweaty if they came up and bit her on the butt.

A tingle went up her spine at the thought of someone, namely Galen, doing that very thing—biting her on the butt. Why on earth would she think such a thing? She didn't have a sadistic bone in her body. When it came to sex, she'd always gone for the traditional. Could that be her problem?

There was definitely one way to find out. She sat on the edge of the bed to think about what was at stake here. First and foremost was ownership of her mother's home. The offer was out there. One week under Galen's roof and he would sign it over to her, free and clear. Of course she would make sure he put it in writing. And then there was the issue of her not liking sex. Nikki was convinced it was her sex partners and not the sex act itself that was to blame. Or it could very well be the incident that happened when she was thirteen that had turned her off sex completely.

If something was wrong with her, then she owed

it to herself to find out and seek professional help if she needed it. After all, she was twenty-eight and most women her age were involved in healthy relationships with men.

At that moment something clicked inside her mind. A sign, perhaps? Was it a coincidence that the house her mother had left her was now tied to Galen Steele? Had fate brought them together if for no other reason than to fix a personal problem she'd tried ignoring? Was Galen, without his knowledge, being used as a tool to right a wrong?

Okay, that thought might be taking things too far, but then, what were the chances of her crossing paths in Phoenix with the same man she'd met six months ago in New York? And then, not only did their paths cross again, but he had something she wanted. Back in New York, she'd had something he wanted—a cab.

She threw her head back. Maybe she was putting way too much thought into this, trying to find excuses to validate what she needed to do. She would be the first to admit that Galen Steele was different from any man she'd ever met. What was there about his brashness and arrogance that pulled her to a different level? All the guys she'd ever dated had impeccable manners, she'd made sure of it. So why was she now drawn to a man whose manners left a lot to be desired?

She reached up and touched her lips with her fingertips, remembering the exact moment he'd kissed her. It had been short but thorough, and she had tasted his tongue. Sensations had jolted her the moment their tongues had touched. None of her former boyfriends were much into kissing. They thought it unnecessary foreplay. But she had a feeling Galen took as much time with a kiss as he did with the sex act itself.

Regardless, it was inappropriate for him to kiss her in a restaurant, and maybe that should be the first thing she covered with him—how he should behave out with a woman in public. It was quite obvious that he was used to doing whatever he wanted, whenever he wanted and wherever he wanted. Her instructions would definitely nip that in the bud.

She felt her heart race at the thought that she had a game plan. Regardless of what he figured he was getting, the only thing she would be delivering to Galen Steele was exactly what he'd asked for, what he definitely needed. A crash course in manners.

And before she could get cold feet, she picked up the phone off the nightstand.

Chapter 7

Galen very seldom went on online for anything other than to check out the competition. But here he was surfing the Internet for information on Etiquette Matters.

A half hour later he couldn't help but smile. What he'd just read was pretty darn cool. In his opinion, Brittany Thrasher was a highly intelligent woman. With an idea she started in college—pretty similar to how he, Eric and Wesley had gotten started—she had created Etiquette Matters. And over the years it had become a very profitable business. According to her bio, she'd had a fascination with the use of proper etiquette and had been considered an Emily Post wannabe. She'd started off with a small column in her university's newspaper and later she gave private classes to young women who'd come from the wrong side of the tracks, had made it to college and were determined to improve their social standing by getting a firm grasp on manners, etiquette and protocol.

She'd found her niche and within a year of graduating she'd hired five people to assist her. Now there were ten in her employ and the business seemed to be doing well. There was always some company or organization that wanted to know the right way to do things. Last year she'd even included a department on international protocol.

She had a waiting list of parents wanting private lessons for their children. And the contract she had snagged with the NFL was definitely impressive. He didn't have to be reminded that she was a professional. The shocked look on her face when he'd kissed her in the café proved that. Any other woman would have been ready to take it to the next level then and there, and would have thought it was a feather in her cap to be kissed in public by a Steele.

But not Brittany Thrasher. She'd been concerned they'd behaved inappropriately. He'd never forget the look on her face when he'd brought up the idea of her teaching him bedroom manners. It didn't take much to make her blush whenever he discussed a couple being intimate, which made him wonder about her sexual experience.

He tapped his fingers on his desk, thinking his mother would probably like her because Eden Steele was big into all that etiquette sort of stuff. She thought the women he was drawn to didn't have any class. How would his mother react knowing he had the hots for a woman who not only had class but was a master at teaching it to others?

He glanced at the clock on the wall. She had only a couple of hours left to call and he honestly didn't think she would. If that kiss hadn't scared her off, then he was certain the discussion of bedroom manners definitely had. The only thing he could hope now was that once she got home and found the package she'd realize the proper thing to do would be to at least call and thank him for his generosity. And when she made that call he would be quick to suggest they get together when she returned to Phoenix to take ownership of the house. From there he'd move things forward.

A short while later, he had finished getting dressed for dinner at his parents' house when the phone rang. He quickly picked it up because he was expecting a call from Eric.

"Yes?"

"I will accept your offer, Galen."

It took him a full minute to find his voice. He truly hadn't expected her to accept. "I'm glad to hear that, Brittany." Surprised, as well.

"I'd appreciate it if you'd have your attorney draw up the papers."

He lifted a brow. "The papers?"

"Yes. I want it stated in writing just what I'm going to receive after the seven days."

He pulled in a deep breath. She was concerned with

what she would be getting after the seven days and his mind was already focusing on what he'd be getting *during* those seven days. Horny bastard.

"No problem," he heard himself say. "I'll have my attorney draw up the papers immediately." There was no doubt in his mind he would have to practically kick Eli in the rear end to do it. No matter. Whatever it took.

A part of him—that decent side—figured he should end this farce by telling her that she already owned the house, but something was keeping him from coming clean. Probably the thought of her in his bed.

"When can I come pick you up?" he asked. Already he was feeling aroused. He shook his head. When had he wanted a woman this much? She had him intoxicated. He wished like hell that he could sober up but he couldn't.

"I think tomorrow morning will be soon enough," she said. He felt his stomach tighten in disappointment.

"That will give me time to check out of the hotel and shop for a few items of clothes I'll need. I hadn't planned to stay in town but a few days." Then she added, "You don't have to pick me up because I have a rental car and I prefer keeping it."

He clamped his mouth shut after coming close to saying he preferred she turn the car back in. After all, there might be a time when he wasn't available to chauffeur her and he'd never let a woman drive any of his cars. "That's fine. Here's my address."

"Hold on, let me grab a pen."

Moments later she was back on the phone and he

rattled off his address to her. "If you need directions I can—"

"I don't need directions. The rental car has GPS."

"So I can expect you around noon tomorrow?" he asked, trying to keep the eagerness out of his voice.

"Yes."

"Good, I'll see you then," he said.

"All right, and don't forget to have the papers with you."

"I won't. Goodbye."

He hung up the phone and rubbed a hand down his face. One part of him felt like a total bastard. The other part of him still felt like a total bastard, but a very happy and excited one.

Eli glared at his brother on the other side of his desk. "Whatever you're involved in, Galen, Brittany Thrasher will end up screwing you."

Galen smiled. Hell, he hoped so.

"You're thinking with the wrong head," Eli went on to add, clearly on a roll. "And don't be surprised if that head gets smashed with all of this."

Ouch! Galen couldn't help flinching at that. Like their old man, Eli had a way with words, especially while reminding you there were consequences for the actions you took.

"Just prepare those papers, Eli. She wants them tomorrow."

Eli shook his head, still not ready to let it go. "This

doesn't make sense. She thinks she has to spend a week with you for a house you've already given to her."

"When she finds that out she'll be surprised and happy, now won't she?"

Eli grunted and then said, "Yes, but your ass still might be grass. Women don't like men taking advantage of them."

Galen rolled his eyes. "And those words are actually coming out of your mouth? You, who have more notches on your bedpost than I do."

"Yes, but I got them honestly."

Galen shook his head. Now he'd heard everything. Instead of arguing with Eli, he moved away from his brother's desk and went to look out the window. The gym across the street had closed hours ago.

He and Eli had come straight from their parents' home where everyone had congregated for dinner. All six sons had been present and accounted for, grudgingly or otherwise. Over the years he and his brothers had figured their mother insisted on her Thursday-night dinners as a way to show her sons that although their father had once behaved like them when it came to women, after meeting her all that had come to an end. In other words, she was allowing them to see with their own eyes that a man who'd been known for his whorish ways could fall in love one day, marry and be true to one woman for the rest of his days. Like Drew Steele.

It didn't take long being in their parents' presence to see just how much in love they were. He and his brothers had always known from the time they were able to walk and talk that Drew adored his Eden. And after nearly thirty-five years of marriage nothing about that had changed.

But what his mother refused to understand was that in her sons' eyes, she was one in a million. The woman who'd brought Drew Steele to heel. She was in a class by herself and there wasn't another woman like her. But most important if there was, the Steele brothers weren't looking for her at the moment. They enjoyed their womanizing ways. There were benefits to not settling down with one woman, but Eden Steele refused to see that.

"Here."

Galen turned his head. Eli had prepared the paper and was holding it out to him.

He couldn't help but smile. "Thanks, man," he said, taking the paper and scanning it. The wording was simple and legal. All he had to do was sign it.

"Whoa, hey, you owe me big. And don't think you won't get billed. For after-hours services, too."

"Whatever."

"And I'm beginning to question your logic when it comes to women, Galen. Are you sure this woman doesn't mean anything to you?"

Galen lifted his head and glanced over at his brother. "Very funny. She's a woman. They all mean something to me."

Eli rolled his eyes. "I'm not talking about *all* women. I'm referring to this particular one. Brittany Thrasher.

The one you signed over a house to. The same one whose name I've seen a lot over the past couple of days."

Galen was silent for a few moments and then he leveled with his brother. "Okay, she's different, Eli. I can't put my finger on why, but I need this week with her."

"To teach you manners?"

Galen smiled. When he'd spelled out the terms of the agreement to his brother, Eli had looked at him like he was crazy. Any son of the eloquent and sophisticated Eden Tyson Steele had impeccable manners. Whether he displayed them or not was something else.

"Manners and whatever else she wants to throw into the class sessions," Galen replied.

Eli rubbed his jaw. "Hmm, maybe I need a class in manners, as well."

Galen's eyes darkened. "Don't even think it. We've never shared before and we won't be doing it now. If you even make an attempt, *my* head won't be the one that will get smashed. Yours will. I'll personally see to it."

Eli laughed. "Sounds like someone has acquired a jealous streak."

"Think whatever you want. Just remember what I said."

A few minutes later, after leaving Eli's office, Galen got in his car and stretched his neck to work out the kinks. He did not have a jealous streak. If anything he had a protective streak. Who wouldn't after hearing the tear-jerking story Brittany had shared with that other woman? He knew the story, although he'd eavesdropped to hear it.

He knew what the house meant to her, her biological mother's last gift, and although he had a reputation when it came to women, he still had a heart. He could still be compassionate when it came to some things, thanks to having Eden for a mother. So for him to have signed the house over to Brittany made perfect sense. At least to his Eden Steele genes. On the other hand, pursuing Brittany for the purpose of sharing his bed was true to his father's genes.

Galen knew he and his brothers had been blessed to have their parents. Brittany had never known her mother, and the house was her only connection to the woman. Seeing her come so close to losing it had brought out protective instincts in him. It didn't matter that he never knew he'd possessed those protective instincts until now. If any of his brothers had been placed in the same position, they would have done the same thing....

Well, maybe not.

The important thing was that he was the oldest and he needed to set good examples for the others to follow. And he'd told Eli the truth. As much as he and his brothers joked around, when it came to certain things, they were dead serious.

Eli thought he was thinking with the wrong head.

Maybe he was. If so, he needed to know why Brittany Thrasher had such pull on not only that part of him but his common sense, as well. He needed to know why he'd thought about her all evening through dinner, and why he couldn't wait to see her tomorrow at his home.

The thought that she would be with him for an entire week filled him with an emotion he didn't understand, and he figured the only way to understand it was to be around her. Spend time with her.

Oddly enough, as much as he wished otherwise, his mind and body didn't transcend into a sex-only mindset when he thought about her. He chuckled as he put his car into gear and headed home. No wonder Eli was concerned about him. The bottom line was that he had invited Brittany to his home to be his lover. He knew it and she knew it.

Knowing it made an unfamiliar sensation settle deep within him, and for some reason he welcomed the feeling.

Brittany tilted her head back to gaze up at the house. The sprawling two-story Tuscan-style structure sat on a hill with the mountains for a backdrop and looked like something that would be showcased in a magazine for the rich and famous.

Although Nikki said all six of the Steeles were successful, Brittany didn't have a clue what Galen did for a living. It was quite obvious that whatever he did paid well.

She glanced around the house and figured it had to be sitting on at least four acres of land. Fittingly, the house had sort of an arrogant look about it. She could see

Galen living here, making this place his castle, his home on the range, his haven against the outside world.

And he was bringing her here to it.

To spend a week with him. Although he claimed she was supposed to teach him manners, she knew what side of the bread was buttered. To get her mother's house she had to be his lover for seven days.

The thought of that had bothered her until she'd talked to Nikki again. They'd had breakfast that morning. "Remember you'll be there for therapeutic purposes," Nikki had said. "No matter why he thinks you're there, Brittany, you're going to use this week to find out some things about yourself. You need to know if there's more to your inability to enjoy sex than what you think."

With that belief firmly planted in her head, Brittany told herself she was on a mission. She needed to see if there were hidden pleasures in her life and if so, Galen was just the man to find them. She was well aware that he had a mission as well—getting her into his bed. Wouldn't he be surprised to discover it wouldn't be as hard as he'd thought? But like Nikki had said, it was only for therapeutic purposes.

She began walking up the walkway when suddenly the huge front door, which looked to be made of solid maple, was flung open. And there he stood, in his bare feet with a pair of jeans hanging low on his hips, and an unbuttoned shirt that showed a hairy, muscular chest and broad shoulders.

"You're early. I just got out of the shower," he said, leaning in the doorway.

She could tell. Certain parts of his skin still looked wet and he had that unshaven look. And as she continued walking toward him, that spark of attraction that had taken hold of her senses six months ago, amidst all her anger and frustration, was back. She'd never experienced anything like this before. Maybe Nikki was right with her hidden-pleasures theory.

He was watching her approach with those deadly green eyes pinned directly on her. He looked as good as good could get and was stirring something within her with every step she took.

"Yes, I'm early," she found her voice to say. "I didn't need to shop for as many items as I'd thought I needed." She felt butterflies in her stomach flapping around. She hadn't known until him that a man's presence could do that to a woman. The idea slid over her and for some reason she felt good about it. Maybe what she'd heard about his abilities was true. A part of her hoped so. She would hate living the rest of her life denying the part of her that was woman.

She came to a stop in front of him. A combination of soap and man plus the scent of cactus gave him a masculine aroma. She studied his face. There was a firm set to his jaw, and the smile on his lips, best described as predatory, only added to the activity going on in the pit of her stomach.

"Come on in. I'll get your things later," he said, stepping back to allow her entrance. "First, I want to show you around and then I want you to relax."

She glanced back at him. "Relax?"

"Yes, you're uptight. I can feel it."

Brittany didn't understand how he could feel anything, but he was right. She was uptight. Who wouldn't be under the circumstances? She had dated Samuel Harold a full six months before they'd slept together and Gilford even longer than that. And here she was, contemplating sharing Galen's bed when he was a virtual stranger. It didn't matter one iota that their paths had crossed six months ago. That time meant nothing and the words they'd spoken to each other had been cross ones.

"I promise not to bite."

A thought occurred to Brittany and she had to fight not to laugh out loud. But she couldn't stop her gasp when she stepped over the threshold and looked around his house. If she'd thought the outside was beautiful, the inside was downright gorgeous. The Venetian plaster ceiling along with the hardwood hickory and stone flooring looked extravagant in a rustic sort of way. And the design of the travertine stairway was an artistic dream come true.

He led her from the formal foyer into a huge living room with a fireplace. She glanced up. The Venetian ceiling in this room was dome shaped and the back wall was made of glass, a wall-to-wall window that provided a forever view of the majestic Black Mountains and the pristine northeast valley.

"There's a fireplace in all the bedrooms," he was saying. "And a view of the Black Mountains can be seen from every room."

He glanced over at her when he said, "But my bedroom gives the best view of all."

Brittany kept looking around, refusing to acknowledge what he'd said. Had he added that tidbit for a reason? She followed while he gave her a tour of the downstairs, which included a spacious kitchen with granite countertops and stainless-steel appliances, a wine cellar, a huge family room, three guest bedrooms, three bathrooms and an office.

Brittany was impressed with his furniture as well as how orderly everything was. She followed him up the stairs and tried not to concentrate on what a nice backside he had in his jeans. As soon as she reached the landing, she let out a sigh. A huge floor-to-ceiling window in the hallway afforded a panorama of the mountains. The view was breathtaking and one you captured as soon as your feet touched the landing.

She could only stand there and stare out.

"I know the feeling," Galen said, smiling. "Sometimes in the evenings I stand in this very spot and watch the sun go down. The rugged terrain makes you appreciate not only the land but the entire earth."

He gestured to a telescope that was mounted in front of one of the windows. "Normally on a clear day you can see up to ten miles with the naked eye, but I use that when I want to see farther than that. I've seen a number of bobcats, mule deer, coyotes and fox. It's quite interesting to observe them in their habitat."

"I can just imagine," she said. Back home she'd seen plenty of sunsets over the Gulf of Mexico. It, too, had taken her breath away. But the only wildlife she'd seen were the ones at Busch Gardens.

She turned her attention away from the view and back to Galen. She hadn't known he was standing so close and tried to avoid looking into the depths of his green eyes by lowering her gaze to his chest. That wasn't a good thing because his shirt was open and all she could see was a sculpted hairy chest. Neither Samuel nor Gilford had hair on their chests and she wondered how it would feel for her breasts to come in contact with it. Or better yet, how it would be to peel off his shirt and then trail her lips down his chest, all the way to where the hair line flowed below the waist of his jeans.

Heat stained her cheeks and she snatched her gaze back to his face, not believing she'd thought of such things. She nervously licked her lips and couldn't help noticing how his eyes followed the movement of her tongue. The way he was looking at her mouth reminded her of their kiss yesterday. It had been short, but it had left a lasting impression on her.

"So what else is up here?" she asked after feeling a tightness in her chest.

He leaned down and placed his mouth near her ear to whisper, "Right now I couldn't care less about what's up here except me and you."

She figured had she been capable of speech he might not have made his next move. But she hadn't been able to talk with the warmth of his breath close on her skin. And when she tilted her head to look up at him, he took that opportunity to swoop his mouth down on hers.

This kiss was a lot different from the one yesterday. She still detected a sense of hunger, but it was as if he'd decided he had no reason to rush. They didn't have an audience and she was not going anywhere. It didn't take long for her to realize that he wasn't just kissing her. He was consuming her, every inch of her mouth and then some.

He angled his mouth in a way that provided deeper penetration and swirled his tongue with hers. And then her tongue started doing something it had never done before: it began mating with a man's. Her world started to spin and she felt grateful when he wrapped his arms around her and brought her body closer to his. Through her blouse her nipples pressed against the cushion of his hairy chest, and just the thought of the contact had her moaning deep in her throat.

Before she realized what he was doing, he had backed her against a wall while his lips and tongue continued to engage hers in a deep, hungry kiss that threatened to push her over the edge of madness. She wrapped her arms around his neck, kissing him back while blood roared like crazy through her veins.

She would be the first to admit she was experiencing some of those hidden pleasures Nikki had warned her about. They were coming out of hiding and she seemed incapable of concealing them again. Whether she liked it or not, she couldn't deny how Galen was making her feel. She stirred with an emotion she had never felt before. Passion. And she knew he was pushing her toward pleasure that only he could deliver.

But it was pleasure she wasn't quite ready for.

She broke off the kiss and pulled in a deep breath. He leaned over and kissed the corners of her mouth. "Is there a reason you stopped it?" he whispered against her moist lips. And it was then that she noticed his hand was underneath her skirt, actually on her thigh and squeezing it. How had it gotten there without her knowing it?

"Is there a reason you started it?" she countered. The man made seduction a work of art.

He lifted his head and smiled. Those green eyes were sexy as sin, totally irresistible. "Yes, there is a reason. I got a sample of you yesterday and I liked the way you taste and couldn't wait to kiss you again." His voice was so husky and deep, goose bumps were beginning to form on her arms.

"Do you always say what you think?"

He flashed an arrogant smile. "I always say what I feel. No need holding anything back."

She doubted he could do that even if he tried. He had the ability to render a woman mindless, make every cell and molecule in her body suddenly feel wicked. It would have been so easy to let him take her right here. Get it all over and done. But a part of her knew her experience with him would not be like the others. There would be no "over and done." He would take her slowly and deliberately. She would feel things she'd never felt before. Be driven to want to do things she'd never done before. And heaven help her, she wanted the experience. Yet at the same time she needed more from him. She needed to know more about him.

"You can let go of my thigh now, Galen."

"You sure?"

"Positive."

He let go and took a step back, and her traitorous thigh was tingling in protest from the loss of his touch. "Come on, let me show you the rest of the house. And just in case you're wondering about that kiss, the answer is no, I didn't get enough."

He led the way and she followed thinking, neither had she.

Chapter 8

Galen kept walking, very much aware of Brittany beside him. He had expected her to ask for the legal papers of their agreement before she entered his home, but she hadn't.

And she hadn't seemed bothered by the impromptu kiss. He could tell she had enjoyed it as much as he had. A part of him wished she hadn't stopped things. No telling what they might be doing now if she hadn't. He could imagine them getting downright naughty and raunchy, hot and sweaty, and tearing off each other's clothes, doing it against the wall and then moving right to the floor.

"How long have you lived here?"

He glanced over at her the exact moment she was pushing a lock of hair out of her face. The brightness of the sun coming in through the window was making her squint, but he thought at that moment she had to be the most beautiful woman he'd ever seen. In a way he found that hard to believe because he'd been involved with a number of gorgeous women in his lifetime. He still found it rather strange that Brittany Thrasher hit him on such a visceral level.

"I've lived here for four years," he replied. "Although my partners and I have a suite downtown, it's only for window dressing to make our business appear legit. Few would imagine we do most of our work out of our garages."

She glanced over at him. "What kind of work do you do?"

"I design video games."

"Video games?"

He turned to her, studied her features to decipher what she was thinking. His occupation got mixed reaction from people. Those who didn't know about the millions he made annually considered his occupation frivolous, certainly not a career a man of thirty-four could take seriously. Of course no one in his family agreed with that assessment, especially because they knew the vast amount of his wealth as well as the hard work it took to create and design a successful video game.

"Yes," he finally said. "That's what I do for a living."

He'd noticed that a smile would first start in her eyes and then extend to her lips before spreading over her entire face. Understandably, he hadn't seen that side of her in New York and hadn't really seen much of it here, except for when he'd witnessed that little reunion with her friend at the auction mart. Now he was seeing it again and the transformation sent his pulse throbbing.

She lifted a brow. "So, are you any good?"

He couldn't help but throw his head back and laugh. This woman was something else. He really liked her spunk once she stopped being angry and uptight.

"Well, are you?"

He shook his head as he finished off a chuckle. "There aren't too many things I'm not good at, Brittany."

She frowned. "It's not nice being conceited, Galen."

A smile touched his lips. "Bad manners?"

He could tell she was fighting hard not to return his smile when she replied, "The worst."

Their gazes tangled and he had to admit he was enjoying the moment. "I guess that's something I need to work on."

"I suggest that you do. Now back to the video games. Are there any out there that have your name attached to them?"

He started walking again and she fell in line beside him. There was something comforting about having her here with him. "There are a few. You ever heard of Time Capsule?"

"Yes."

"What about Wild Card?"

"Yes, I've heard of that one, too."

"And what about Turbine Force?"

"Of course." She stopped walking and turned to him. "Are all those yours?"

"All those are SID's, a corporation that I own along with two college friends. All three of us can claim success of the company."

"See there," she said as a huge smile touched her face. "You're a fast learner. You could have been conceited and taken all the credit for the success of your company, but you didn't. You shared the spotlight. You remembered your manners. I'm proud of you for doing so."

Galen shook his head. For the first time in a long time a woman had left him speechless.

So instead of saying anything, he began walking again while wondering for the first time what he had gotten himself into.

Brittany couldn't help but notice that Galen had suddenly gotten quiet on her. Just as well because she needed to think a minute. One thing she'd learned over the years was to respect another's need for a quiet moment. So while Galen seemed to be indulging in his, she glanced around, thoroughly pulled in by the appeal of his home.

It had a charm about it that spoke volumes. Whether Galen realized it, his house revealed a lot about his personality. A segment of it at least. She doubted very few, except those close to him, knew the real Galen Steele.

She'd never considered herself an outdoorsy person, but evidently Galen was. Most of the paintings on his wall indicated his appreciation for nature, in that they captured the natural beauty of the outdoors. And then she couldn't get over the view outside the window they were walking by. It literally took her breath away. In Tampa she was mostly surrounded by water, but here in the desert, she was surrounded by mountains. Mountains out of which Galen had mapped his space. One he was comfortable with. One that was totally him.

He stopped when they came to another room and she did likewise. When he stood back she stepped inside. It was another bedroom and Brittany thought it just as nicely furnished as the others she'd seen so far.

She glanced over at him. "You have a lot of house for only one person."

"I like my space."

She'd figured as much and wondered if he was giving her a hint. But then she dismissed the idea when she recalled that her being here was his idea. She had offered to stay at the other house, but he'd turned her down.

Moments later after showing her three other guest bedrooms, several spacious bathrooms and an upstairs library stacked with numerous books and video games, they walked down a hall that jutted into a wing that was basically a separate extension of the house.

Galen glanced over at her and said, "In addition to my space I also like my privacy. I have five brothers and once in a while we get together and play video games until dawn. When I want to retire for the night I prefer not hearing their excitement from winning or their strong, colorful expletives from losing. They tend to be rather rowdy."

"You and your brothers are close."

"Yes, although we pretend not to be at times. Tends to be more fun that way and with us, there's never a boring moment, trust me. Our parents are our rock. They have a strong marriage, a solid one. And I think what I admire about them most of all is that they're best friends."

"That's impressive."

Galen nodded. He'd always thought so, and he knew his brothers had, as well. But to hear an outsider confirm it pretty much validated their feelings. He hadn't asked her anything about her family and he couldn't help wondering if she found that odd. No odder than her not asking for those papers when she had insisted on them just last night. He couldn't help speculating why.

He pulled in a deep breath wondering if she knew how good she smelled. He guessed it didn't matter, because he did. He covertly studied her profile and wondered why he was even bothering when he was used to openly checking out any woman he was interested in. Any woman he wanted. But he wanted to watch her when she wasn't aware she was being watched.

It didn't take long to decide the side of her looked just as nice as the front. Her nose seemed rather short, but her full lips made up for it, and when you tacked on a sexy-looking chin, what you got, in his opinion, were nearly flawless features.

His gaze returned to her lips and lingered, and he remembered the feel of them pressed against his while he took her mouth in a kiss that even now had him aching. He was so engrossed in her lips that it took him a moment to realize they were moving and she was asking him a question.

"Excuse me?" he asked.

She met his gaze and there was an inquiring look in them when she repeated her question. "Does this door lead to your bedroom?"

He then noticed they had reached his bedroom door. "Yes, this is my private haven, but I give you permission to enter it at any time."

She gave him a weak smile. "Do you?"

"Yes." He wanted to reach out and touch her, to see if this moment was real. Had he really just given her something he'd never granted another woman—the right to invade his space whenever she wanted to? That was so totally unlike him.

He opened the double doors and then stepped aside. He wanted to see her reaction. He smiled when she glanced around, totally in awe of his bedroom. It had a masculine overtone while at the same time captured so much of the outdoors with the one solid wall of glass that showcased the beautiful mountain scenery. And then there was his see-through ceiling where he could wake up any time of night and look up at the stars.

He followed her gaze up after seeing the look of astonishment on her face. At that moment he could imagine her sharing his bed beneath those same stars. He would love making love to her one night while lightning flashed in the sky or the rain poured down.

He had seen such a ceiling in his travel to Paris one year and knew he had to have one for his own. When he had the house built, this ceiling was the first design he made sure was in the plans.

"This is truly awesome, Galen. I've never seen anything like it before. I bet sleeping in here is an adventure."

He could only smile at that assumption. "Yes, you can say that."

He then watched as she crossed the room to take a closer examination of his bed. His bedspread was white, not the usual color a man would choose, and he hadn't. His mother had. In fact after buying the house, he had gone skiing one week to come back and discover she had decorated his bedroom.

It had taken a while for the white coverlet to grow on him and those days when it didn't, he would swap it out with a black one he kept in one of the closets. This morning while making the bed he'd decided to go with the white, thinking it would make a better impression. He propped against his bedroom door wondering when he started caring about making an impression on a woman.

He looked at her and knew it had been since meeting her. His first impression hadn't gone over so well, so now he was trying to win her over. That was even more so unlike him.

There was a momentary silence as she turned around slowly, taking it all in, the furnishings and the view outside the window. She then turned to him and said, "This room is simply beautiful."

"I'm glad you like it. This is where you will sleep every night while you're here."

She stared at him. "Why do you want me in here?"

Without taking his eyes off her he moved away from the door. There was no way he would tell her that the thought of having her in his bed was an arousing one, even if he wasn't in that bed with her. "Do I really have to go into details as to why I want you in here, Brittany?"

She broke eye contact and looked out the window. She returned her gaze to his and said, "No."

"Good. Now if you'll excuse me, I'll go bring in your luggage."

Chapter 9

Brittany stepped back from the dresser after placing the last of her unpacked items into the drawers. She glanced around the bedroom, still amazed at what she saw. She'd honestly never seen anything like it. Even the furniture was massive, as if specially made for a giant. On one side of the bed was a foot step to use when getting into the bed because it was so high off the floor.

She glanced up and saw the sky in all its brilliant blue. Galen had shown her the switch to use when she wanted a sliding shade to block the view, but she couldn't imagine not wanting to lie in bed and stare up into the sky.

He had delivered her luggage to her and without saying anything—other than telling her about the switch and indicating the top two drawers for her use—he'd left her to her own devices.

She figured he was having one of his quiet moments or he was one of those moody people who preferred being left alone when they had a lot on their minds. But because he was the one who insisted that she come live with him for a week, she assumed he wouldn't mind the company. She headed downstairs.

She didn't have to go far to find him. He was in the kitchen. At some point he had buttoned his shirt, but his jeans were still riding low on his hips and he was once again barefoot. He looked both sexy and domesticated standing at his kitchen sink.

"When can I go check out the house?" she asked.

It was easy to see from his expression that he hadn't known she'd been standing there and he waited a moment before he replied. "I'm ready when you are, but I'd think you'd want this."

He picked up a legal-size envelope from the table and handed to her. "It's the papers you demanded yesterday."

She took the envelope from him and pulled out the legal document and read it silently. Everything was as it should be. She placed it back inside the envelope and glanced over at him. He had returned to the sink. "Your brother is your attorney?"

"Among other things. Usually a pain in my rear, mostly. But I can say the same thing about the others, as well. Being the oldest isn't all that it's cracked up to be."

He glanced at his watch and said, "I guess now is as good a time as any to check out that house. We can stop somewhere on the way back and grab lunch."

She smiled. "All right. I'll just go upstairs and get my purse."

Galen watched as she hurried toward the stairs. He knew why that house meant so much to her, but she didn't know that he knew, and for some reason he wanted her to feel comfortable in telling him herself. He drew in a deep breath thinking he'd much prefer staying here and getting something going with her, but he knew the best thing to do was to get them out of the house for a while. Just the thought that she would be sleeping in his bed, whether he was in it with her or not, had his heart beating something crazy in his chest.

He'd been close to the breaking point when he returned with her luggage and found her standing there, still checking out his bed. There had been something about the overwhelming look in her eyes that touched him in a way he'd never been touched before.

And that wasn't good.

"So tell me about your brothers, Galen."

Galen briefly glanced across the seat of the car to meet her inquiring gaze. After she indicated that she preferred they take the rental car, he suggested that he drive. He'd promised himself never to let another female behind the wheel while he rode shotgun after an angry Jennifer Bailey had taken the Sky Harbor Expressway at over one hundred miles an hour—all because he refused to make her his steady girl. He didn't care that he'd been a senior in high school at the time. Some things you didn't forget.

He tilted his Stetson back from his eyes. "Why do you want to know about them?"

"Because there seems to be so much unity among you, even though the six of you might disagree sometimes. I lived in a foster home while growing up and although there were a number of us, unity didn't exist. It seemed everyone had their own separate agenda."

"And what was yours?"

She hesitated a moment before answering. "Survival, mostly. And hoping the people who were my foster parents would want to keep me. I hated moving from place to place, making new friends, attending different schools. There was no stability."

Anger flashed within Galen at the thought that she'd never grown up with real parents, siblings or a home to call her own. Now more than ever he was grateful he'd made the decision to turn her mother's home over to her. Still, he wanted her to talk to him. Tell him why the house meant so much to her.

"Is that why you wanted that house so much?" he prompted. "Did you live there at one time as a foster child? Did you—"

"No," Brittany said, interrupting his questions. "That's not the reason."

She paused, then said, "I wanted the house because it was willed to me by someone I've never met. My birth mother. She gave me up for adoption when I was born.

Only thing is, I never got adopted. Most of the people who took me in did so for the extra income. I have to say I was treated decently the majority of the time, so I won't complain."

She paused for a moment before continuing. "Six months ago…in fact, it was the same day I saw you and returned from New York. When I got home, I discovered I'd gotten a letter from a woman informing me that she believed I was the daughter she'd given up for adoption twenty-eight years ago, and that I would be hearing from her again soon with arrangements for us to meet if I wanted to do so. There was no return address and that's all the letter said. I anxiously waited, and last week I received a letter from an attorney letting me know that my mother had passed away and had left her house to me."

She paused again. He'd come to a traffic light and glanced over at her. She was staring straight ahead. "It was only when I got here and met with her attorney that I found out about the back taxes on the house. Her taxes got delinquent because she used the money to hire a private investigator to find me. She had been diagnosed with cancer and was given five years to live. She found me, but we didn't get the chance to meet face-to-face."

She drew in a deep breath and glanced over and met his gaze. "So now you know the reason I want that house."

Yes, he knew, Galen thought. He'd known all along. At least the part he'd overheard when he should not have been listening. He was silent for a long moment and was grateful when the traffic light changed and the car moved forward. He needed to concentrate on his driving and not on the woman sitting beside him. She was doing strange things to his emotions and Galen wasn't so sure he could stop them.

Brittany swallowed hard and her heart beat furiously in her chest when Galen brought the car to a stop in front of the house that used to be her mother's home. She couldn't move, so she just sat there and gazed at it through the windshield. The first thing she noted was that the windows were no longer boarded up.

She glanced over at him. Her brow furrowed. "You've been here already?"

"No. Once I got your call yesterday afternoon I contacted someone to come take the boards off the windows. This is my first time seeing it."

She nodded. He'd said from the first that the only reason he'd bid on the house was because she'd wanted it. Galen Steele had proven that he definitely had an ulterior motive for owning this home now.

"Ready to go in?" he asked.

Her throat closed and she could barely get out her response. "Yes."

By the time she had unbuckled her seat belt, he had already gotten out of the car and walked around to open the car door for her. She was discovering that Galen used good manners and could be the perfect gentleman when it suited him.

They didn't say anything as they headed down the

walkway. The moment she stepped onto the porch she saw up close what she hadn't seen from a distance. The house could use a paint job and the screen door needed to be repaired. She couldn't help wondering if these repairs, too, had taken a backseat to hiring a private investigator to find her.

Brittany paused for a moment to take in the enormity of what she was feeling, the emotions deep within her that had risen to the surface. Would she find answers to all the questions she had? Would she ever know why she'd been given away? Who was her father? Had he even known about her?

"You okay?"

She glanced up at Galen. She might have been mistaken, but was that concern in the depths of his green eyes? "Yes, I'm fine. Thanks for asking."

He reached into his pocket and pulled out a single key. "Here, the house is yours."

She raised a haughty brow. Did he assume because she was here at the house today that she would be in his bed tonight? "Jumping the gun, aren't you?"

He gave her an arrogant smile as he removed his Stetson. "No, I don't think so. Come on, let's go inside."

For a moment Galen stood back and watched as Brittany entered what had been her mother's home. He then followed her inside, closed the door behind them and glanced around. The interior looked a lot bigger than the exterior but everything inside, from the

Early American–style furniture to the heavily draped windows, had a sense of home.

His gaze moved over to Brittany. She was no longer standing in the middle of the floor but had moved over to a vintage-looking desk and was looking at a picture in the frame. Deciding not to stare, he glanced around again.

It was evident that although the outside showed signs of deterioration and neglect, the interior did not. Everything looked well cared-for and maintained, even the hardwood floors. It was clear that the person who lived here believed in being clean and neat. The place gave off a feeling that its owner had merely stepped out a minute and would be returning momentarily.

"Nice place," he said to Brittany, mainly to get her talking again. She'd gone too quiet on him and continued to stare at that picture frame. Was it a picture of the woman who had been her mother?

When she didn't acknowledge his remark, he knew she had effectively tuned him out, although not intentionally because her manners wouldn't allow such a thing. Emotions had taken over her, and he wasn't used to dealing with emotional women. Usually that was when he would cut and run like hell. But he wouldn't be going anywhere today. He felt as if he had a vested interest in this woman, which really didn't make much sense. All he wanted was to get her in his bed so she could soothe the ache in his pants. What he didn't understand, and what he was trying like hell to figure out, was his insane fascination with her.

And at the moment he didn't like her wandering around this place sinking deeper and deeper into a maudlin state of depression he refused to accept for her. He'd rather have her mad than sad. But right now he wanted her talking.

She glanced over at him and the look in her eyes was like a kick in the gut. It was as if he felt her pain. She hadn't known the owner of the house, nor would she recognize her if they'd passed in the street. But none of that mattered. The woman who used to live here had been her mother. The woman who'd given birth to her.

The woman who, for some reason, had given her away.

He waited for her to say something. The look in her eyes said she was ready. He wasn't Dr. Phil by any means, but he figured she needed to express her feelings, get them out in the open.

"I think I look like her," she said, holding the picture out for him to see.

He moved away from the door, crossed the room and took the picture frame she offered. He studied the image of the woman standing beside a tall man. She looked younger than Galen had expected, which meant she'd had Brittany at an early age. Probably a teen pregnancy. "Yes, you do favor her," he said honestly. "I wonder how old she was when she gave birth to you."

"Sixteen. According to her attorney she died at forty-four."

He nodded as he handed the picture frame back to her. "You want to check out the other rooms?"

"Sure."

She walked slowly and he did likewise beside her. The kitchen was nice and the bay window provided a view of a lot of the land. It seemed to go on for miles. And the view of the mountains was just as impressive as the one from his place. No wonder those men at the auction mart wanted to demolish the house and build a hotel on the land.

He walked around the kitchen to the table. Just like the rest of the house, the table and chairs were Early American and fit perfectly in their setting.

Brittany then moved to the window and was looking out at the mountains and all the land. He decided to keep her talking.

"Do you know if she had any other relatives?"

She turned around. "According to her attorney, Mr. Banyon, she didn't. She and her husband never had any children. I'm not even certain he knew about me."

She moved away from the window and placed her hands on her hips and his gaze was immediately drawn to that area of her body. He liked how she looked in that skirt and figured he'd probably like her even better without it. Without a single stitch on her body. Okay, he would admit he was an ass, without a lick of manners. Here she was mourning the loss of her mother and his mind was in the bedroom.

"I guess we need to see the rest of the place," she said, lacking enthusiasm and reclaiming his attention. When she crossed the room to pass by him he got a whiff of her. Her scent had nearly driven him crazy on the drive over and it was playing havoc with his senses again.

There were two bathrooms, both of which he'd consider remodeling if the house was his. But it wasn't. He recalled her reaction when he'd handed her the key and told her the house was hers. Of course he'd meant it because legally it was. But the look she'd given him told a different story. She'd no doubt figured he'd given it to her because of the terms of their agreement. She was so far from right it wasn't funny.

"Thanks for having those boards removed, Galen. The view from every window is fabulous."

The midday sun was pouring through the windows of every bedroom they passed and seemed to hit her at every angle. There was just something about a beautiful woman. Now they stood in the master bedroom. It was a little larger than the other bedrooms and it did have its own bath. Brittany was standing next to the bed. The king-size and oversize furniture seemed to take up most of the space, making it tight to walk around much. Just as well. It wouldn't take much to tumble her onto that bed about now. It looked so inviting and she looked so damn enticing.

"Do you know what your mother did for a living?" he cleared his throat and asked, deciding to stay where he was standing in the doorway.

She looked over at him. "Mr. Banyon said she'd been a librarian within the public school system for years."

He nodded. "That doesn't surprise me. She was probably prim and proper just like you."

She tilted her head and met his gaze. "You think I'm prim and proper?"

"Yes. Don't you?"

She frowned. "No. I just believe a person should display good manners."

He glanced around and then looked back at her. "And I'm sure you're going to think I have atrocious manners when I say that I feel we've been here long enough and that I'm ready to go."

"But we just got here. You could leave me for a while and return for me later."

He could but he wouldn't. He wanted her with him, if that didn't sound crazy. It wasn't that he didn't have anything to do. He had Sniper to work on. But right now the only thing he wanted to work on was her. Tomorrow he'd probably feel differently and would give her a chance to come over here by herself to go through her mother's stuff. But today he couldn't handle her sadness any longer.

"That's not our agreement, Brittany. I brought you here so you can check out the place and we've done that. It's past time for lunch. Do you have a taste for anything in particular?"

He could tell from the expression on her face that she hadn't liked being reminded about their agreement. "No, wherever you decide is fine."

He was glad she wasn't pouting or pitching a fit

because they were leaving. There had been enough gloom for one day, and he wanted to take her someplace to put a smile on her face.

Chapter 10

An hour later they had returned to Galen's home and Brittany was rubbing her stomach. "I can't believe I ate that much. It's all your fault."

Galen chuckled. "It was my fault that you made a pig of yourself?"

"That's not a nice thing to say."

He rolled his eyes. "Okay, Miss Manners, it might not be nice but it's true."

She dropped down on his sofa. "Maybe next time you'll think twice before taking me to an all-you-can-eat place that serves barbecued ribs that fall off the bone."

He shrugged. "Then I'm not a good man," he said as if the thought didn't bother him in the least. "Earlier you schooled my manners on being conceited. Do you have any other lessons for today?"

"There are a couple I'd like to interject."

He took the armchair across from her. "Go ahead."

He was sitting right in her line of vision and a part of her wished he wasn't. Her reaction to him today wasn't good. She had handled it pretty well at her mother's house, because her mind had been filled with so many other things. But at the restaurant, she had been filled with images of him. So much so that her nipples pressing against her blouse had throbbed through most of the meal. And now there were these nerve endings inside her that seemed pricked, painfully stretched, whenever those laser green eyes lit on her.

He was leaning back in the chair, his legs crossed at the knees in a manly pose. His thighs were taut and his abs sturdy, masculine and ripped beneath his shirt. She felt a tingling in her fingers. They itched to reach out and touch his bare skin. She'd bet his flesh would be warm. How would it taste? Heat drenched her face. She'd never thought of putting her mouth on a man before.

She cleared her throat and forced her attention back to business. "Your cell phone," she said.

He lifted a brow. "What about it?"

"You answered it in the restaurant."

A smile touched his lips. "I answer it wherever it rings. That's why they call it a mobile phone. It's a phone on the go."

She rolled her eyes. "Proper etiquette dictates that you should turn your cell phone off in a restaurant just like you would do at church." From the look on his face she got the distinct impression that he didn't turn his phone off in church, either. Or maybe the look meant he didn't go to church.

"And if I miss a call?"

"You'll know it and you can call the person back once you leave the restaurant. Was it someone you couldn't call back later?" In a way she didn't want to know. What if it was a woman he was interested in?

"It was Mercury being nosy."

"Mercury?"

"My brother."

She nodded and tucked her legs beneath her on the sofa. She noticed his gaze followed her every movement. "You have a brother named Mercury?" she asked.

"Yes, and before you ask, the answer is no, he wasn't named after the planet or that Roman god. He was named for Mercury Morris. Ever heard of him?"

"Of course. I'm from Florida. He was a running back for the Miami Dolphins in the seventies, during the time they were unstoppable, undefeated one season."

She watched him smile and wanted to roll her eyes. Did men think they were the only ones who knew anything about football?

"My father was a huge Dolphins fan while growing up," he said. "He still is. In fact, he got drafted right out of college to play for them, but a knee injury kept that from happening before the start of what should have been his first season."

"How sad."

"Yes, it was for him at the time." He paused a moment and then said, "Okay, I get the 'no cell phone in the restaurant' rule. What's the other?"

She shifted in her seat when his gaze drifted down to her breasts and she wondered if he'd noticed her hardened nipples through her blouse. "The other is toothpicks. I didn't see you use them and I'm glad for that, but several others in the restaurant did. You don't stick a toothpick in your mouth after finishing a meal."

"We had ribs."

"That makes it worse," she said.

"But they're on the table."

"I noticed. Usually there're at the cash register on your way out. There's nothing nice about a person using a toothpick to pick their teeth at a restaurant, especially when others are still eating. You should take the toothpick and use it in the privacy of your own home."

He leaned forward in his seat. "And you know all this stuff, how?"

She smiled. "I studied it in college. I got a degree in history, but I took every course offered on etiquette and even saved my money for Emily Post Finishing School a couple of summers."

He nodded and stood up, and her gaze traveled the length of him. He was tall, well over six foot, muscular and his body was honed to perfection. He had an abdomen with a six-pack if ever there was one. She was so enraptured by him that she barely heard him say, "So I read on the Internet."

She raised a brow. "You looked me up on the Internet?"

He smiled. "Of course. You said you had a business and I wanted to check it out to make sure you were legit. I was impressed. So now I know for sure that you know what you're talking about."

He glanced at his watch. "I have some things to do in my garage. You can decide on dinner when I return in a few hours," he said as he was about to move away.

"Wait," she said. "Is that it? That's the manners lesson for today?"

His gaze then swept over her and she felt the heat emanating from the dark orbs wherever they touched. A sardonic smile then touched his lips when he said, "Yes, but there's always tonight. You can get prepared for whatever manners you want to go over with me then."

She lifted her chin. "That sounds like a proposition."

She saw irritation flash in the depths of his green eyes. "The proposition was made days ago. You accepted and as a result you're here under my roof. Mine for seven days to do as I please. And nothing will please me more than to have you naked in my bed beneath me every night while I breathe in your scent and make love to you until we both reach one hell of an orgasm."

She gasped at his words and she suddenly felt breathless. Her knees weakened and she was glad she was already sitting down or she would have fallen flat on her face. An image of her naked in bed beneath him flashed through her mind, and she was filled with a wanting she'd never known before.

His voice had deepened to a husky tone and he'd spoken promises he intended to deliver. He evidently didn't believe in holding back on anything, even words that a true gentleman wouldn't say, words that put her out of her comfort zone. She'd never dealt with a man like him before. He not only stated what he wanted, but he was letting her know he intended to have things his way.

And maybe that's exactly what she needed.

A man who was arrogant, sure of himself, a pure alpha male through and through. One who had manners when they counted and refused to display them when they didn't. She fought the inclination to cross the room and kiss him, which at that moment seemed the most natural thing in the world for her to do. Her, of all people. A woman who before meeting him would never have considered doing such a thing.

But Galen Steele had a way of pulling something out of her, and like Nikki, she was now convinced if there were hidden pleasures lurking somewhere beneath her surface, she would know about it before she left his home seven days from now.

She slowly stood up and placed her hands on her hips, tilted her head back and gave him what she hoped was one hell of a haughty look. With a man like him, a woman needed to be able to hold her own. "Talk is cheap, Galen. We'll see later how well you are on delivering."

She inwardly smiled. The effect of her words was priceless. Although he tried to keep his emotions in check, she read the look of startled surprise in his eyes. He hadn't expected her to goad him.

Brittany pulled in a deep breath when he began walking toward her, but she refused to step back or move away, although her heart was beating a wild rhythm in her chest. He didn't need to know her hands were trembling on her hips and heat had gathered at the juncture of her legs.

"You're right, Brittany, talk is cheap," he said when he came to a stop in front of her. The sound of his deep, husky voice made those already-hardened nipples get even harder.

"But I won't be doing much talking and neither will you. I believe in action."

She swallowed. "Do you?"

"Very much so. And just so you know, I want you. I wanted you in New York and I definitely want you now. And I'll give you fair warning. Tonight is taste-you night. I want the taste of you in my mouth, all over my tongue and embedded in my taste buds when I wake up in the morning."

Brittany's stomach clenched. This man of Steele was making her hot merely with his words. He hadn't touched her yet. And now he would taste her? Just the thought was filling her with more desire and longing than she'd ever felt before. She suddenly became fully aware of something that was new and exciting to her. Carnal greed.

She swallowed. "Like I said. Talk is cheap."

He smiled in a hungry way. "And like I said, I'm a man of action."

Then he leaned in and captured her mouth, not giving her a chance to stifle the moan that immediately rose in her throat. His arms wrapped around her, and his hands stroked her back at the same time his tongue stroked every inch of her mouth.

She had long ago decided his kisses were unique, full of passion and capable of inciting lust. But she was also discovering that each time they kissed, she encountered a different effect. This kiss was tapping into her emotions and she was fighting like hell to keep them under tight control where he was concerned. This was all a game to him. Not for her. For her, it was about finding herself in more ways than one. Discovering her past and making headway into her future.

He deepened the kiss and she felt his hands move downward to cup her backside and pull her more fully against him. She groaned again when she felt his hard erection press into her at a place that was already tingling with longing. Unfamiliar sensations were floating around in her stomach and she was drenched even more in potent desire.

And then he suddenly broke off the kiss and took a step back. She watched him lick his lips as if he'd enjoyed kissing her and then he thrust his hands into his jeans pockets, looked at her and asked, "Did I make my point?"

Oh, he'd made it, all right, but she'd never admit it to him. "Kind of."

She quickly scooted around him. "I think you should get to work now. I plan on setting up my laptop and answering a few e-mails. And then I plan to work on tomorrow's manners lesson for you." She headed toward the stairs.

"Brittany?"

She stopped and turned around. "Yes?"

A smile touched both corners of his mouth. "I like you." His face lit up as if the thought of it was a revelation to him or something.

She rolled her eyes. "Should I be thrilled?"

He gave her an arrogant chuckle. "The thrill will come later."

She turned back toward the stairs and damn if she wasn't looking forward to her first orgasm ever.

Chapter 11

Galen shut off the lamp on his worktable. Surprisingly, he had gotten a lot done once he'd been able to put Brittany to the back of his mind.

He liked her.

He had told her that earlier and had meant it. There were no dull moments with her around. Just when he thought he had her figured out, she would do or say something to throw him off base, literally stun him. His Miss Manners was becoming a puzzle he needed to put together, but there were so many pieces, he wouldn't know where to start. One thing was for certain, she was definitely keeping him on his toes.

Just like he had plans to keep her on her back starting tonight.

He smiled at the thought and leaned back in his

chair as he recalled their meal at the restaurant earlier today. There was nothing like a buffet that included mouthwatering ribs and the best corn bread you'd ever want to taste. Jennie's Soul Food drew a lot of truckers, businesspeople and just plain everyday folks. Brittany hadn't been bothered by the mixture of clientele. The last woman he'd taken there had complained all through dinner, saying she'd felt out of place. That had been their first and their last date. He hadn't looked her up afterward, not even for a booty call. Personally, he didn't like women who whined or who felt they had a reason to complain about everything. Brittany was definitely not that type of woman.

He glanced at his watch. It was six already, which meant he'd been holed up in his garage for at least four solid hours. He'd still managed to get a lot done while anticipating tonight's events. He wondered if Brittany had taken his advice and was prepared. Probably not. He had pretty much spelled things out to her earlier. Laid them on the table, so to speak. Given her the real deal. If there had been any doubt in her mind just what his proposal had been about, now she knew. But he was certain she'd known all along that her being here was not just about teaching him manners. Oh, he was enjoying her little tidbits and would certainly keep them in mind, but manners weren't all he intended for them to cover over the next seven days.

He wondered where he would be taking her for dinner. Wherever they went he wanted to make sure she again ate well because she would definitely need her strength for later.

Galen stood to stretch his body and immediately felt his erection kick in. He was hard. He was ready. And it was time to find his woman. *His woman?* Okay, it had been an unwitting slip. He didn't think of any woman as his. But in a way Brittany was his—at least for the next seven days. After she left, his life would get back to normal. He was sure of it.

It was a romantic setting straight out of a movie. Brittany drew in a deep breath as she glanced around the bedroom. She'd taken all the advice the Internet had to offer. After checking e-mails from her staff, she'd searched several Web sites on what to do for a romantic night. Then she'd put the bedroom together.

She had every reason to believe Galen would deliver tonight and if he did, it would be her first orgasm ever. She wanted more than just the bells and whistles; she wanted drums and several trombones, as well. She would have a lot to celebrate after twenty-eight years, and she just hoped and prayed things came through for her. The thought that she was emotionally damaged from her teenage trauma was a lot for her to take in.

She glanced at the clock on the nightstand and wondered how much longer Galen would be working in his garage. A couple of times she had started to go find him, but figured he might not appreciate the interruption. Besides, she'd needed to prepare for tonight.

Deciding she wouldn't be kept a prisoner, she had scribbled him a note and given him her cell-phone number so he would know how to reach her. And she'd taken off to shop for everything she needed for tonight. Because he hadn't tried reaching her, chances were he hadn't known she'd left.

In addition to purchasing scented candles, she'd also bought a bottle of wine and a dozen red roses whose petals she'd strewn over the bed. Then there was the racy new outfit guaranteed to escalate her seduction.

She felt a deep surge of nervousness as she glanced down at herself. Talk about being bold. She'd never owned a pair of stilettos until now. And red of all colors. She had paid good money for them, although she figured she wouldn't get much use out of them after tonight. According to the online article, men wanted sex frequently and they liked seeing their women looking sexy—preferably naked and wearing stilettos.

Brittany had decided she could go with the stilettos, but she would definitely not be naked. Instead she'd purchased the short red dress she'd seen in one of the stores' window. Like the shoes, it was a first for her. She had the legs to wear a hemline halfway up her thighs, but she worried that if she were to bend over in this dress, Galen wouldn't miss seeing much. Including her new red lace panties.

She drew an unsteady breath, wondering if perhaps she'd gone a little too far. But then she had to remind herself there was a reason for her madness. Not only had she gotten her mother's home out of the deal, but she would also find out tonight whether she was frigid.

She shuddered at the use of that word but knew she had to call it what it was or could possibly be. According to the research she'd done on the Internet today, that word described any woman who didn't have a sex drive. She fit into that category.

However, she believed all that would change tonight. Already she felt a deep attraction to Galen and he had been able to get her juices flowing, literally. But the last thing she wanted was for him to question why she was so eager to become intimate with him now after she'd resisted his offer initially. He didn't need to know that in addition to wanting her mother's home she had a hidden motive for accepting his offer. A secret she'd shared only with Nikki and one she would take to the grave with her.

In addition to turning his bedroom into a seduction scene, she'd made a pit stop at the grocery store after discovering his pantry bare. Another rule of manners he'd broken. She wasn't Rachael Ray by any means, but she didn't do so badly in the kitchen. And just in case the sex thing with her was a total flop, at least she'd have the meal as a consolation prize.

Her ears perked up when she heard the sound of a door closing and figured it was Galen coming out of the garage. She nervously nibbled on her bottom lip knowing at any moment he would be coming up the stairs for her. She knew what happened after that would determine her fate.

Whatever it took—even if it was every ounce of resolve she had—she would get through it. No matter the outcome.

Galen sniffed the air the moment he closed the door from the garage. He had to be at the right house, but couldn't remember the last time he'd encountered the smell of food cooking.

He walked into his kitchen and glanced around. He'd been living here for four years, and this was probably the first time his stove had earned its keep. And the only thing his refrigerator had been good for was to chill his beer because he ate out one hundred percent of the time. Getting a home-cooked meal at his parents' place was one of the reasons he actually looked forward to Thursday nights.

He glanced over at his table. It was set for two with elegant china, silverware and glasses. He then glanced back at the stove and saw all stainless-steel pots. He could only assume all this kitchenware belonged to him. Was it a house-warming gift from his mother when he'd first moved in? Now that he thought about it, he was sure of it.

Whatever was in those pots sure smelled good and he couldn't wait to get into it. But then he frowned. If for one minute Brittany assumed a home-cooked dinner would replace the sex they were to have later, then she had another thought coming. He could get a meal from just about anywhere.

Galen turned toward the stairs, bracing himself for

what he figured would be opposition to keeping her side of their agreement. She had been the one who'd tossed the "talk is cheap" challenge out there, and he was so looking forward to hearing her give one hell of an orgasmic scream. He could just imagine his hard body intimately connected to her soft one, her arms wrapped around his neck or her hands gripping his shoulders. All that mattered was getting inside her, thrusting in and out. His penis, which had gotten hard from the moment he'd finished working that day, seemed to have taken on a life of its own. If he didn't know better he'd suspect it had Brittany's name written all over it.

He'd never been this hard up for a woman. Each step he took up the stairs, closer to her, made his erection surge in anticipation. The lust that had been eating at him, nipping at his heels, from the first time he'd set eyes on her had overtaken his senses, was devouring his control and intoxicating his mind.

Galen wasn't sure what he would do if he'd discovered Brittany had reneged. He didn't expect her to be already naked waiting for him in his bed, but he didn't expect for her to come kicking and screaming, either.

He moved toward the hall that led to his bedroom, not sure what he would find. It wouldn't surprise him if he found her sitting with her laptop still working on her e-mails. He knew there hadn't been any food in the house, which meant she had gone to the grocery store at some point. No doubt she wasn't happy about doing that.

He placed one foot in front of the other thinking this

had to be the longest walk of his life, mainly because what awaited him on the other side could make or break him. He should never have allowed any woman to sink her claws into him this deep. But he'd been a goner the first time she'd frowned at him when he'd hijacked her cab. And he hadn't been right in the head since.

When he stood in front of the closed double doors to his bedroom, his eyebrows furled. Was that music he was hearing? He reached out to open the doors and then quickly remembered his manners. Although it was his room, for the next seven days they would be sharing it and he had to afford Brittany the courtesy of knocking before entering. Pulling in a deep breath, he tapped his knuckles on the door.

"Come in."

He lifted a brow. Was he imagining things or had he heard a tremble in her voice? Taking another deep breath, he opened the doors. What he saw made him blink and mutter in a shocked tone, "Holy crap."

Chapter 12

Galen was convinced his heart had stopped beating, his lungs had seized and his penis had doubled in size. He had to literally shake himself just to get his body back to working order.

Brittany stood there with a sexy smile on her gorgeous face, and the "come get whatever you want" invitation he saw in her eyes suddenly made him feel like Adam in the Garden of Eden. Only thing missing was the apple.

"It took you long enough to get up here, Galen."

He swallowed. If she hadn't said his name he would have wondered if she was talking to him. Was she saying she'd been waiting for him to make an appearance? What the heck was going on and why did he feel he had gotten caught in some sort of trap?

In his peripheral vision he saw that his room had

been transformed into a setting he hadn't ever seen before. Candles, imparting the scent of vanilla, glowed all around the room, soft music was playing and red rose petals were sprinkled over his bed, giving the room an overall romantic effect. He'd never thought he had a romantic bone in his body—until now.

But what caught his attention and held it more than anything was Brittany herself. How in the hell had she known that a woman in stilettos was his weakness, especially if she had legs like hers? And if that wasn't bad enough, the stilettos were red.

It was her dress, however, that had his erection throbbing, his tongue feeling thick in his throat. Where in the hell had she gotten something like that from? It was red to match the shoes and it was short. The fabric crisscrossed at the top and tantalized at the bottom with its flirty hem that barely covered her thighs. What was she trying to do? Kill him?

That thought, quite seriously, sent all kinds of questions flying through his mind. But all it took was a whiff of whatever perfume she was wearing to lay them to rest unanswered. His main consideration was getting her out of that dress.

"So how did work go today?"

He blinked, realizing she had spoken, and then what she was asking. While heat drummed through him, he figured that he needed to move his tongue to answer. "I finished my goal for today. Just one or two more pieces to work on this week and I'll be ready."

None of what he said was making any real sense.

His mouth was saying words that his body didn't comprehend. Finish what? Ready for whom? His mouth was merely responding to her inquiry when the rest of him wanted to respond in another way. Forget the small talk.

"I didn't know you were waiting for me," he said, moving toward her, deciding to dispense with preliminaries and anything keeping him from her. Manners be damned.

"Yes," she said. "You probably didn't notice, but I left for a while to do some shopping. Because I'd found your pantry bare, I also stopped by the grocery store to pick up a few things to prepare for dinner. Rule number four is to never invite someone to your home as an overnight guest without plans to feed them."

"I was going to take you out," he defended.

"For breakfast, lunch and dinner?"

"Yes."

"Don't you ever cook for yourself?"

"No."

"That can get kind of pricey," she pointed out.

"I can afford it," he said, coming to a stop in front of her. "Is this dress real?"

"Touch it and see," she challenged.

"I think I will."

Galen smiled and for one heart-stopping moment, Brittany suddenly realized he wouldn't stop at touching the dress. He reached out and his hands slowly made their way down the front of her dress, tracing his fingers across the soft material. But as expected, his hands didn't stop there.

They slid over the softness of her shapely figure, as if molding her in a way that made her breath choppy. When he took a step closer and cupped her buttocks, rubbing his hands over their firm curve, she fought back the moan from deep within her throat.

"What is this about, Brittany? Why are you all of a sudden handing yourself to me on a silver platter?" His voice was husky as his hands continued to roam.

She stared into the depths of his green eyes. "You ask too many questions," she said in a voice that trembled even to her own ears. He was standing close. His body was pressed into hers. She could feel the outline of his erection through his jeans. His eyes were trained on her face, causing goose bumps to appear on her arms and stirring a hunger within her. A hunger that was all new to her.

Deciding it was time to be bold and take things to the next level, she wrapped her arms around his neck and molded her body to his. She felt her already-short dress rise up in the process. Air fanned her butt as she pressed her hardened nipples into his solid chest. Instinctively, she shifted her body, causing her hips to move against his rock-hard thighs and his very aroused penis.

The thought that he wanted her filled her head with an excitement she'd never felt before. It made her bolder. Made her want things she'd never desired before. Made her want to do things she'd never done before.

She decided not to fight anything tonight, to just roll

with the flow. Let loose. Be something she'd never been before—one of those sexually needy chicks. And with that thought in mind, she stood on tiptoes and offered her mouth to him.

He took it, and the thrust of his tongue between her lips made her quiver. At the same time that his mouth ravaged her, his hands took advantage of her raised dress and began caressing her backside and then slipping under her lacy panties to touch her bare skin.

He continued to kiss her in a way that made her moan and spread heat through all parts of her body. The juncture of her thighs tingled. Nothing she and any other man had done in the bedroom could equate to this. A mere kiss. Never had she gotten fired up to this degree. Or to any measure, to be honest. She hated admitting she used to pretend in the bedroom. Actually she'd gotten pretty good at faking it. But there was nothing bogus going on here.

Their lips clung and she wasn't aware until now a mouth could actually make love to her. It was as if he was determined to know her taste, emerge himself in her scent. He seemed content just to stand there, feel her body wherever he liked and explore her mouth. And she was pretty much content to let him. They had kissed before, but never like this. Never with this much hunger, greed and intensity.

He suddenly broke off the kiss and the sound of his breathing—rapid successions of quick, hard breaths—matched her own. He met her gaze and held it and she noticed his lips were wet from devouring her.

"You do know this dress is coming off, don't you?" he asked in a deep, throaty voice.

"And what if I said it was glued to my body?" she teased.

He smiled. "Then I would have to prove that it wasn't. Stitch by stitch. Inch by inch." And he began doing just that as his hands slowly moved over her body, tugging the dress off her shoulders and down her hips.

She heard his sharp intake of breath when he saw her red lace bra. And with a flick of his wrist he undid the front clasp and let the bra fall, setting free her twin mounds. His mouth immediately set upon them, drawing a nipple into the contours of his mouth to begin sucking.

Brittany grabbed hold of his shoulders when she felt weak in the knees. She hadn't known her breasts were so sensitive. Hadn't known they could ache for a man's mouth, until now. He had moved his mouth to the other breast, and quickly he had latched onto the other nipple, sucking profusely, and causing her stomach to tighten with every pull.

Holding her nipple hostage, he tilted his head to gaze up at her and she saw a flicker in the depths of his eyes as his hands remained clenched around the curves of her buttocks.

He lifted his head, touched his lips to her neck when he whispered, "Remember I told you it was 'taste you' night." And without waiting to see if she recalled it or not, he dropped to his knees in front of her. "I want the taste of you in my mouth. We're going to see just how cheap talk is, baby."

Brittany tried to ignore his term of endearment when she lifted her heels to step out the dress that had tangled around her feet. He tossed it aside and glanced up at her wearing nothing but red lace panties and red stilettos.

"Damn, you look sexy. And tasty," he said, leaning forward, his hot breath right there at the crotch of her panties. He reached out and slowly began easing them down her legs and over her shoes to toss them aside.

He leaned back on his haunches. She was standing in front of him naked except for her high heels. When she made a move to take them off, he said, "Leave them on."

She looked at him questioningly, but only for a minute. His hands had slid up the backs of her thighs, while his face had moved close to her stomach. He was licking the flesh around her belly button. The feel of his tongue on her stomach sent unfamiliar sensations through her, flooding all parts of her. And then, in a simultaneous invasion, his hands cupped her backside at the same time his mouth lowered to her womanly folds. He slid his tongue between them, and Brittany let out a deep whimper.

Never had any man tasted her there. But he wasn't just tasting her. He was devouring her. She grabbed hold of his shoulders as his mouth seemed intent to make a meal of her. She deliberately rolled her hips against his mouth, instinctively pushed forward as blood rushed to her head, making her dizzy.

His hands held her buttocks, determined to keep her pressed to his mouth as his tongue filled her, sent widespread shivers through her. She continued to whimper as he ravaged her womanhood, openmouthed and thrusting deep, as far as his tongue could go.

This was what other women had experienced. Why they kept wanting more. Why they'd looked at her like she was crazy when she seemed oblivious to what an orgasm was about. Now she was finding out firsthand. She felt it building, right at the juncture of her thighs, under the onslaught of Galen's mouth and tongue.

The throbbing between her legs intensified until it was downright unbearable, and then suddenly her entire body ignited in one hell of an explosion and she cried out his name and catapulted in a free fall. This was pleasure. One of those hidden pleasures that Nikki had warned her about. The intensity of it held her captured within its grip.

How had she gone twenty-eight years without experiencing this? The cells in her body felt pulverized and she succumbed to every novel feeling, soared higher than she'd ever thought possible.

When she thought she would crumble to the floor, he pulled his mouth away, stood and swept her off her feet into his arms. He moved up the steps to the bed and placed her on it, right on those rose petals and among the scented candles. And then he moved back, stared at her stretched across his bed. Naked, except for her shoes.

At the questioning look in her eyes, he said, "Keep them on. It's my fantasy."

And then she watched as he began removing his clothes.

Chapter 13

Galen unbuttoned his shirt thinking there was no woman he wanted to make love to more than the one stretched out on his bed, naked except for those sexy red high heels he dreamed about.

He'd asked her to keep them on because he'd never made love to a woman with her shoes on, and because the ones she was wearing looked so damn hot on her. Too hot to take off. He'd seen women in sexy heels a number of times and had always gotten one hell of a boner. But seeing Brittany in them was messing not only with his body but also with his mind.

He couldn't take his gaze off her. She was lying on her side facing him and her breasts were full, firm and high and the nipples he had sucked on earlier looked ready for him to feast on again. And then there were the dark curls between her legs, looking as luscious as anything he'd ever seen. He was getting harder just looking at that part of her. Using his mouth, he had made her come. And before the night touched the stroke of midnight, she would come plenty more times.

As he tossed his shirt aside he tried to come to terms with what was going on with him where she was concerned. Why was she so embedded under his skin that he was intent on screwing her out of it?

He swallowed hard at the thought of that tactic backfiring on him and instead of screwing her out of it, he might just bury her deeper into it. But for some reason that possibility didn't bother him. He breathed in deeply, feeling antsy, unreasonably horny. Maybe he ought to slow things down a bit.

For what purpose? his mind snapped back and asked. She was in a giving mood tonight, so he'd best just take what she was offering.

His erection had thickened and lengthened, and like a divining rod, it was aimed straight toward her, namely the juncture of her legs. He removed the rest of his clothes and when he stood naked in front of her, he let out a deep growl when her scent reached him. And from her scent, he knew she wanted him as much as he wanted her.

But something was nagging his mind, making him wonder why she was being so generous tonight. She had known when she'd accepted his offer that it would come down to this. Still, she hadn't been happy about it. Why had she done a one-eighty?

"Manners rule number five, Galen. Never keep a lady waiting."

Her words made his heart pound and his pulse race. And as he moved toward the bed he knew that she *was* a lady. The sexiest lady he'd ever met. "There's a good reason for this delay, sweetheart," he said, moving to the bench at the foot of the bed. "A must-do." He lifted the top and pulled out a condom packet and proceeded to sheath himself.

He knew she was watching his every move. When he finished, he braced one knee on the bed, held out his hand and said, "Come here, baby."

He thought her movement was as graceful as a swan, and she looked sexier than any woman had a right to be. When she reached him and placed her hand in his, he leaned toward her and began placing kisses up the side of her neck while whispering how much he wanted her.

He then began trailing kisses along the curve of her shoulders, liking the taste of her skin there just as much as he had the area between her thighs. The sweet taste of her womanly essence was still on his tongue and would stay there for some time. And then he kissed her deeply as they tumbled backward onto the bed together.

It was then that Galen pulled back and stared deep into her eyes. "I need to know," he whispered. "I need to know that tonight isn't a fluke and tomorrow you'll regret everything that takes place in this bedroom. And even worse, that you won't share yourself with me the next six days."

He outlined her lips with the tip of his finger. "Tell me that won't happen, Brittany."

Brittany stared deep into Galen's intense eyes and at that moment she doubted she could deny him anything. Not this man who'd less than twenty minutes ago given her the experience of her first orgasm. And for that she was exceedingly grateful. The last thing she would have tomorrow was regrets. Nor did she want to deny herself this pleasure for the next six days. She was a late bloomer where sex was concerned, but tonight she'd become a woman finding out how to lose herself in the heat of passion and pleasure.

"Tell me, Brittany."

She swallowed. A part of her silently warned she was getting in too deep. She should take tonight and be done with it. Anything beyond this could lead to some serious trouble. What if he discovered it had been more than the lure of her mother's house that brought her to his bed? That it had also been her quest to find out more about herself. Her need to know if she could enjoy an amorous relationship with a man.

He'd proven she could. Should she take that knowledge and run? Be through with it? Let him know there wouldn't be any more sensual interludes between them and all he would be getting from her over the next six days were lessons in manners? She knew she wasn't capable of running anywhere. Now that he'd revealed all her hidden pleasures, she wanted to spend as much time as she could and explore those pleasures with him.

"There won't be any regrets tomorrow, Galen," she said in a soft voice. "And I'm committed to keeping my end of our agreement, so there will be more nights like this one."

He frowned and she wondered why he was doing so. Hadn't she just stated what he'd wanted to hear? They both had their own ulterior motives for sharing this week. He'd been right when he'd said that he had something she wanted and she had something he wanted.

But what happened after the seven days?

A shiver ran through her, although the answer to that question was simple. He went his way and she went hers. She would have her mother's home and he'd get his week of sexual enjoyment. What more could either of them expect?

She tilted her head and studied Galen, wondering the reason for the heavy silence. "That's what you want, isn't it?"

"Of course."

Still, she continued to look at him, wondering if she was missing something. She shook off the possibility that she was. Before she could dwell on it any more, he lowered his mouth and captured hers again.

Galen, she decided, was a perfectionist when it came to kissing. Some of the things he did with his tongue should be outlawed. Even now he was sucking gently on hers, while his hands were touching her everywhere, squeezing her breasts, teasing the hardened tips of her nipples. And then he lowered his hand between her legs and inserted a finger into her.

She pulled her mouth back and drew in a deep breath before burying her face in the warmth of his hairy chest. He smelled good. He smelled of man. And his intimate touch was driving her sensuously insane. When his free hand moved to caress the slope of her back she lifted her head from his chest and met his intense gaze.

"Make love to me, Galen."

She whispered the words not caring that her request probably lacked manners. The protocol was changing, and women were bold enough to ask something like that. Still, such an audacious request sounded strange coming from a female. However, at the moment the only thing she cared about was the deep ache in her stomach that had been there for a while and had become unbearable the moment he'd removed his pants to reveal the thatch of dark curly hair at his groin. There was just something about seeing him exposed and the thickness of his erection that had heat radiating to her lower limbs. She wanted him in a way she'd never truly wanted a man. With Galen she could be herself. She could be the woman she'd never been.

She wanted him. He wanted her. And for now that was all that mattered.

"Be careful what you ask for, sweetheart," he whispered as he gathered her close to the warmth and solid hardness of his body. She felt his arousal pressed against her belly and was compelled to reach down and grip his manhood in her hand.

She remembered touching Gilford once and the harsh words he'd said when she did. He'd reminded her that she was a lady who was above doing such things. Instead of being turned off by her actions, it was evident Galen had no such problem with her touching him, if the sound of his heavy breathing and deep guttural groans were any indication. Empowered by his response, she began stroking him, liking the feel of the thick veins that outlined the shaft of his penis, and the warmth that emitted from the tip of it.

"Damn, Brittany," he growled. "You're about to make me lose my manners."

She smiled thinking he just had. A true gentleman would never swear in front of a lady. Instead of pointing that out to him, she decided to inflict her own brand of punishment by sinking her teeth into his shoulder blade and then licking the bruise with her tongue.

"Payback, Brittany."

He shifted their positions and she found herself flat on her back with him looming over her, sliding in place between her open legs and red stilettos. And she knew whatever patience he'd been holding in check had gotten tossed to the wind. She glanced up at the see-through ceiling. It had gotten dark and there were stars in the sky adding to the romantic effect she'd created.

That effect stirred everything within her and when she felt his manhood at the entrance of her mound, nudging her womanly folds apart trying to seek admittance, streaks of anticipation flooded her.

Then she felt him, the heat of him sliding inside her wet channel, stretching her, taking her, preparing to mate with her. Her muscles clenched him, gripped him, needing something only he could give. She knew she had to relax, stop being greedy, but this was all new to her and she wanted it all.

He remained still when he was inside her to the hilt and then he glanced down at her and whispered, "Wrap those legs and high heels around my waist. I want to feel you. I want to feel them. I'm about to do the very thing to you that those shoes stand for."

And he did.

He began moving in and out of her, and the throbbing between her legs intensified with each stroke. She did just as he suggested and wrapped her legs around him, stilettos and all.

He lifted her hips to receive him deeper and she could actually feel blood rushing through her veins. And then in a surprise move he lowered his head and captured a nipple in his mouth and began sucking while his body rode her hard. She bit her lips against a moan and then gave up and screamed out his name when a mass of sensations ripped through her.

She pressed closer to him, tightened her legs around him as he continued to pound into her. Heat burst into flames and she tightened her grip on him when he bucked several times with whiplash speed. They held nothing back. They shared passion, pleasure and possession. Tonight he was hers and she was his. He kept thrusting inside her until he had nothing left to give, and then finally he moaned her name and collapsed on top of her.

When his breathing returned to normal, he shifted

his weight off her. She cuddled closer to him as if that was where she belonged.

He laid a hand across her thigh as he met her gaze, breathing in deeply and then saying, "That was simply amazing. Incredible." He then reached down to remove her shoes and tossed them across the room.

She lay there, completely sated, as she tried to catch her breath. She totally agreed with him. She wondered what he would think if he knew tonight was the first time she'd made love and considered it a pleasurable experience.

He wrapped his arms around her and pulled her closer. "Let's sleep a while. Dinner will keep until later. Besides, I doubt either of us has the strength to get out of this bed right now."

He was right, she thought, laying her head on his chest and giving in to her body's exhaustion. She felt drained, yet at the same time flagrantly and passionately pleasured. She moved her head to look at him, and when she did their eyes locked. He had been looking at her. At that moment something passed between them. Just what, she wasn't sure.

Sensations rippled through her all over again and she knew at that instant that Galen Steele was every woman's fantasy.

He was certainly hers.

Chapter 14

Brittany woke up the next morning, shifted her body and stared up into the sky. She could even see birds flying overhead through the bedroom ceiling. Amazing. She closed her eyes thinking nothing was as amazing as making love with Galen last night.

She had lost count of her orgasms. After they'd taken a nap and awakened to make love again, they had slipped into their clothes and gone downstairs to eat, totally famished.

Galen told her more than once how much he enjoyed her spaghetti, which she'd served with a salad and garlic bread. He had even asked for seconds. Then he had helped with the cleanup. The next thing she knew, she was swept into his arms and taken back upstairs where he'd made love to her again several more times.

She'd come close to telling him what last night had meant to her and how her better judgment had warned her against the indulgence. But Galen was a man used to sleeping with women who know the score, and although she wasn't a virgin, her experience left a lot to be desired. In the end, she kept the secret.

She shifted in bed and wished she'd stayed put when her muscles ached. The intensity of Galen's lovemaking last night had made her sore, which would no doubt slow her down a bit today. At least until she took a hot, relaxing bath. Then she would go over to her house. After yesterday she finally allowed herself to label the house as hers, especially after Galen had given her the key.

She wondered where he'd gone. Although today was Saturday, he was probably downstairs working in his garage. She had yet to see that part of his house and knew he considered it his private domain where he allowed his creativity to flow. She smiled thinking his creativity had done a pretty good job flowing right here in this bedroom last night.

Easing out of bed, she went into the bathroom. If Galen intended to work all day today, then she could very well revisit her house. If he thought she would be at his beck and call, then he had another think coming.

Galen's heart began racing when he heard Brittany moving around upstairs. Although he'd been tempted to wake her early this morning to make love again, he'd figured she needed her rest, especially because he'd kept her up most of the night.

He probably should feel like an oversexed, greedy ass, but he was too damn satisfied, far too content, to find fault in his behavior last night. Besides, he knew although Brittany might not have expected to go as many rounds with him, she'd enjoyed each and every one of them. Her screams were still ringing in his ears.

Something about her screams, though, hadn't been right. Not that he thought she'd been faking them, mind you, but he'd made love to enough women to recognize the tenor of a scream. Listening to Brittany's, one would get the impression she'd never screamed during a climax before. It could very well be that she assumed screaming displayed reproachful behavior, definitely a lack of manners. But still, lack of manners or not, some things couldn't be held back. And letting go while gripped within the throes of passion was one of them.

He moved away from the sink to open the refrigerator and again was taken aback by the sight of the items inside. Milk, eggs, cheese, fruit… The meal Brittany prepared last night had been off the charts. But he hoped she didn't assume she had to cook, because he'd made it clear he had no problems with their eating out. And then there was dinner at his parents' home on Thursday night and—

Holy crap! Brittany would still be here on Thursday night. According to the terms of their agreement that Eli had drawn up, she wouldn't be leaving his place until next Saturday morning. There was no way he would take her to his parents' place for dinner. He didn't want anyone getting the wrong impression, and knowing his mother, she would. It was not the norm for women to hang around his place on a frequent basis. Although several had spent the night, he didn't waste time helping them to the door bright and early the next morning. And it went without saying that he'd never taken a woman to his parents' dinners.

"Good morning."

He hadn't heard Brittany come down the stairs. But then why would he have been listening for her? Talk about irregular behavior...

He drew in a deep breath, closed the refrigerator door and turned around. The moment he did so, a fine sheen of perspiration touched his brow. Some women looked better than others in the morning and he quickly decided she fit in that category. She had taken a shower, which was probably the reason she looked so fresh in her top and jeans. But a shower hadn't put the glow on her face. He had posted enough notches on his bedpost to know only a night of earth-shattering sex could do that to a woman. He inwardly flinched at the thought of her being a notch on anyone's bedpost, including his.

"Good morning, Brittany." There was no need to ask if she'd gotten a good night's sleep because thanks to him she hadn't.

Instead he asked, "Where would you like to go for breakfast?" He had showered and shaved earlier and was ready to go. And getting out of the house wasn't such a bad idea; then he wouldn't have thoughts running through his head of taking her back upstairs.

"I can prepare something for us. Won't take but a minute. At least, if that's all right with you because it's your kitchen."

Yes, it was his kitchen, and as far as he was concerned, everything in it was his, including her. He then heaved a sigh, wondering how his mind could think such a thing. There was no woman alive that was his. He borrowed them for the time it took to get his pleasure and then he returned them to where they'd come from. It would be easy to tell Brittany she could go upstairs and pack, and that starting today she could stay at her mother's place, but for some reason he couldn't fix his mouth to say those words.

Instead he said, "I don't have a problem with it. I just don't want you to assume I expect it of you."

He watched in fascination when her lower lip started to quiver. Call him sick but he had missed seeing that, although he knew she was vexed with him for some reason. "Trust me, Galen. I know your expectations where I'm concerned."

"Do you?"

"Yes."

A sudden smile touched his lips. "In that case…" He moved toward her. As soon as he reached her, he picked her up off her feet and placed her on his kitchen counter and moved between her jeans-clad legs. Already he missed seeing her in those sexy high heels.

"What do you think you're doing, Galen?" she asked, staring at him with a frown on her face.

That elicited a laugh from him. "I bet you won't ask me that in a couple of minutes." He then swooped his mouth down to hers.

Brittany wondered why after a night like last night, they were at odds with each other this morning. And why did it take this, another Galen Steele mind-blowing kiss, to put things in perspective?

Instead of thinking about the answers to those questions, she decided to concentrate on the kiss instead. Might as well, because it would have snatched her focus anyway. Heat always sizzled between them whenever their lips locked and this morning was no exception.

His hands reached up to cup both sides of her face, making her feel the intensity of him making love to her mouth. And that was exactly what he was doing. His tongue was ravaging her, leaving no part of her mouth unscathed.

His mouth continued to move against hers with a hunger she felt all the way to her toes, and she couldn't resist returning the kiss with equal fervor. All she could think about was how last night this same mouth and this very naughty tongue feasted at her breasts and between her thighs, driving her over the brink of madness and lapping her into orgasm after orgasm. Neither could she forget his powerful thrusts into her, over and over, in and out, making her scream more times than she could count. It was a wonder her throat wasn't raw this morning.

He pulled back, breaking off the kiss, and she stared into his face, saw that arrogant smile on his moist lips and she swallowed hard. It was either that or grab his shirt and make him kiss her again.

"Now, you were asking?"

She blinked. *She'd asked him something?* Oh, yeah, she'd asked what he thought he was doing. He'd given her an answer in a tongue-tangling way. Brittany considered saying they should take this to the bedroom but decided not to. Instead she said, "Breakfast. What are we going to do about breakfast? This is Saturday, so I'm sure most breakfast places are crowded and it's after nine already."

He nodded and she noticed his gaze was glued to her lips. "So what do you suggest?"

"I suggest I prepare something. Afterward I'm sure you have your day planned."

"I had thought about putting in more time on Sniper today."

"And I plan to go over to my mother's place for a while."

He lifted her off the counter and placed her back on her feet. "It's no longer your mother's place. It's yours. I gave you the key yesterday and she willed the house to you, so you might want to start thinking of yourself as the owner."

She rubbed her arms where his hands had touched. "I know," she said smiling faintly up at him. "But no one has ever given me anything before." And that had been the truth. Even during the Christmas holidays when she'd received presents from her foster parents, she'd known the gifts had been donated by charity.

He took a step toward her and reached out and traced the curve of her mouth with his thumb. "But all that's changed now, hasn't it?"

He was standing close, so close she could feel his erection through his jeans pressing against her. She couldn't stop the stab of sexual sensations that spiked through her veins.

His question made her realize that yes, it had changed. Her mother may have given her away when she was born, but before Gloria McIntyre had left this earth she had found her and had tried making things right. Not that they had been wrong. A part of her had always figured her mother had been a teenager who'd wanted the best for her. She'd had no way of knowing that what she'd wanted for her daughter and what her daughter eventually got were two different things. But then maybe she did know once she'd gotten the investigator's report.

"Do you need my help?"

She gave Galen a reluctant smile. What she needed was for him to leave the kitchen so she could concentrate. "No, I can handle things. Why don't you go to the garage and start working," she suggested. "I'll call you when I'm done."

"And you're sure you don't need my help?"

"I'm positive."

"All right. And you don't have to come to the garage looking for me. I'll be back up in fifteen minutes or so. I'll lay out my supplies and come back."

He turned to leave, then, catching Brittany off guard, he pulled her against him and covered her lips in a kiss that sent her pulse racing. When he released her, he whispered against her moist lips, "I like you." And then he moved toward the door that led to his garage.

"Tell me about your brothers, Galen."

Galen glanced across the table. When he had returned from the garage, it had been just in time to see Brittany place the pancakes she'd prepared on a platter. Then there were the eggs, bacon and orange juice. Everything he would normally get at Flynn's Breakfast Café where he ate most mornings. But he would be the first to say the meal Brittany had prepared could hold its own against Flynn's any day.

He lifted a brow. "My brothers?"

"Yes."

She had asked about his brothers before, a couple of times, and he'd always avoided her question. His family was his family, and most people living in Phoenix knew the Steele brothers. Most women he'd dated didn't ask about his brothers, because Tyson, Eli, Jonas, Mercury and Gannon had managed to carve out reputations around the city on their own. He had to remember Brittany wasn't from Phoenix, though, which could be a good thing. She wouldn't know about the Steele brothers' reputation. She had no idea some women considered them the "Bad News Steeles." Nor would she know they liked women in their beds, but had no plans to keep them in their lives.

"I mentioned I'm the oldest," he started off by saying. "After me there's Tyson. There's only an eleven-month difference in our ages. At thirty-three he's the doctor in the family, a heart surgeon and a damn good one."

He took a sip of his coffee, thinking it tasted just as good as any he purchased from Starbucks. "After Tyson there's Eli. As you already know, he's the attorney in the family. He's thirty-two. Then there's Jonas, who's thirty-one. Jonas owns a marketing firm and has some top names as clients. After Jonas there's Mercury at thirty. He's an ex-NFL player turned sports agent. And last but not least is Gannon, the youngest at twenty-nine, but he's definitely not the smallest. He took over the day-to-day operations of my father's trucking company and even gets behind a rig himself every once in a while."

He leaned back in his chair. "So there you have it, the Phoenix Steeles."

She smiled and lifted a brow. "There's more?"

He chuckled. "Yes, mostly living in North Carolina. Have you ever heard of the Steele Manufacturing Company?"

"Yes."

"That's those Steeles."

"You're close to them, as well?"

"Of course, they're family."

"Of course."

He looked down into his coffee cup as he recalled

that Brittany did not have a family, and he remembered what she'd said about never feeling a part of any of her foster families. He wished he could have changed that for her.

"So tell me about Galen Steele."

He glanced up thinking he'd rather not. But he would, because talking was a lot safer—he wouldn't be tempted to take her upstairs and communicate in a different way. "What do you want to know?"

"Anything. Everything."

He couldn't help but smile at the thought of that. Either could get the both of them in trouble. "I like sex." He thought the blush on her face was cute. Just as cute as the quivering of her lips when she got angry.

"I know that already. What else do you like?" she asked.

"You. I like you," he said honestly, even though he knew such an admission would rattle her.

He watched her bite her lip. "Yes, I think you've said that already, too," she said. "What else do you like besides sex and me?"

"I like auto racing. The Steele Manufacturing Company sponsors a car for NASCAR, so I travel to the races quite a bit."

She nodded. "When our paths crossed in New York, you were there for a wedding, right?"

He chuckled. She'd made it seem like it had been a casual meeting when it had been anything but. He'd swiped her cab. "Yes, my cousin Donovan. There wasn't supposed to be a wedding."

She lifted a brow. "There wasn't?"

"No, because Donovan wasn't ever supposed to marry. He was supposed to be a bachelor for life."

"Is that what he'd said?"

"Yes. Always."

Galen stared back into his cup of coffee, which was almost empty. Donovan used to say it and was quite serious about it, but a woman had come along and changed his mind. Galen was certain that he would never let that happen to him, and to this day he didn't understand how it happened to Donovan. His cousin had had everything going for him. Any woman he wanted. And then Natalie came along and whammo, he'd fallen in love and the next thing everyone knew, he was talking marriage.

Deciding they'd sat at the table and chitchatted long enough, he stood to clear his plate. "You sure you don't need me to help do anything over at your place?"

"Yes, I'm positive. Today I plan to go through her things and see what I need to pack up and what I want to keep."

"You don't have to do everything in one day, you know."

"Yes, I know. But I want to get it done."

"Well, call me if you change your mind and need my help," he said, taking his plate and cup to the sink.

"You have your own work to do."

Galen was about to say that he didn't care how much work he had to do; if she needed him, he wanted her to call. She came first. But he quickly clamped his mouth shut, wondering why on earth he'd think something like that. No woman came before his work…except his mother and most of the time that couldn't be helped. His father had basically spoiled Eden. She'd been the only female in a houseful of males and she'd been treated like a queen. Unfortunately, she hadn't pulled off her crown yet.

"Just call me if you decide you need me. And don't wash the dishes. Just put everything in the sink. You cooked breakfast, so I'll clean up on my next break."

Growing frustrated over what seemed to be his mounting fascination with her—memories of their night together weren't helping matters—he said, "I'll see you later." And then he left the kitchen.

Chapter 15

Brittany moved around her mother's home. In a way she was glad Galen hadn't come with her this time. She needed space from him to think. For some reason he'd appeared guarded this morning. Although he'd kissed her when he'd sat her up on the counter, from then on he seemed cool. Not cold but cool. She hoped he wasn't thinking she wanted something beyond this week because she didn't. All she wanted was full ownership of this house, fair and square, and then she would decide what she would do with it.

She moved toward her mother's room and pulled out several drawers. There were more pictures of Gloria McIntyre and a man Brittany could only assume was her mother's husband. They seemed like a close pair.

Brittany had decided if she didn't find anything to

give her a clue as to why her mother had decided to look for her all these years, then she would go talk to the private investigator she'd hired. Maybe the man could shed light on a few things.

She pulled out another drawer, thinking like the others she would find more pictures, and was surprised to find a journal. Her heart rate increased as she pulled out the journal and closed the drawer. It was thick and she could tell it contained many entries.

Moving quickly to her mother's bed, Brittany kicked off her shoes before lying down on the bed. One of the first things she'd done when she arrived this morning was strip the bed and put on fresh linen. The washer and dryer were going and she intended to have the sheets back in the linen closet before she left. It was still early yet, not quite four o'clock. More than likely Galen was working and hadn't noticed the time.

The first entry she came to was written eighteen years ago on January tenth. Brittany's tenth birthday.

I tried to bring up the subject of the baby I gave away, my beautiful little girl, but Walter doesn't want to talk about it. He'd said he could handle it when I first told him about her last year, but now I'm not sure I did the right thing.

Brittany quickly sat up. Her mother had told her husband about her? Quickly she scanned ahead to another entry, recorded on her thirteenth birthday.

Today my daughter becomes a teenager. I hope the family that adopted her loves her as much as I do. It was so hard for me to give her up, but I wasn't given a

choice. I couldn't abort her like Mom and Dad wanted.
Especially after Britton drowned. She was to be our
baby. Britton and I had so many plans, and when he
died he left me all alone.

Brittany's heart jumped. Her father's name had been
Britton and he'd drowned. A knot formed in her throat
when she kept reading.

I cried for days and Mom and Dad refused to speak
to me for months, but I wouldn't back down about the
abortion. They finally sent me away to Phoenix to live
with Uncle Milton and Aunt Pauline. I agreed to give
my baby up for adoption since everyone said she would
go to a couple who wanted a baby but couldn't have
one. They would love and cherish my baby like I would
have done. When I met with the people at the adoption
agency a month before my due date, I thought they
were nice, and they said I could even name the baby.
I decided to name him Britton if he was a boy and
Brittany if she was a girl. She was a girl so I named
her Brittany. I got to hold her for only a little while and
I thought she looked like Britton. She was a beautiful
little girl with a head full of curly black hair. I noticed
two of her fingers were crooked and her feet were turned
in but the nurse said they would eventually straighten
out. Happy Birthday, Brittany, wherever you are. I hope
you're happy.

Brittany wiped a tear from her eye. She hadn't been
happy. While her mother assumed she was somewhere
being loved and cherished by some nice couple on her
thirteenth birthday, it had been just weeks after that

when Mr. Ponder had tried to molest her. And those fingers never changed, and as a child she had to wear heavy metal braces that fit into her shoes until her bones straightened out. Both birth defects made her a flawed baby nobody wanted to adopt.

Brittany looked down at her hand. All her fingers were straight now because one of the first things she'd done after making a profit at Etiquette Matters was to have surgery on her fingers.

She drew in a deep breath and continued reading. Seconds turned into minutes and minutes into hours. The entries came to an end and Brittany was so full of her mother's love that she couldn't stop the tears that poured from her eyes. All those years when she thought nobody loved her, nobody cared, here in this house located thousands of miles from where she lived in Florida, Gloria McIntyre had loved her. She had made an entry in memory of her on every birthday she'd had.

Brittany couldn't do anything but drop back down on the bed and cry her eyes out. She understood why her mother had given her up thinking she would get a better life, but still…

"Brittany? What's wrong?"

Brittany snatched her head up and through the tears she saw Galen. Where had he come from? She pulled herself up and by then he was there, pulling her into his arms, and she went willingly, circling her arms around his neck.

"What is it, Brittany?" he asked, his voice soft and

filled with concern as he sat down on the edge of the bed with her in his arms.

And then the words came pouring out and she knew to him they probably made no sense and ran all together. "My mother loved me. My father's name was Britton and he drowned when he was eighteen, leaving my sixteen-year-old mother pregnant with me. My grandparents wanted her to get an abortion but she wouldn't, so they sent her here to live with her uncle and aunt. The people at the adoption agency let her name me after my father, and promised to give me to a nice couple who would love and cherish me. But nobody wanted me because two of my fingers were crooked and I had to wear those metal leg braces until my bones straightened out. And then when she thought I was doing fine on my thirteenth birthday, that was the year Mr. Ponder tried to molest me, which is why I've never liked sex. And I paid a plastic surgeon to fix my fingers. She wanted to find me but had to wait until her husband died and then she died before I could meet her."

There, she'd said it all and then she cried even more. And Galen just held her.

It wasn't supposed to be this way, Galen thought as he stared into space while holding the woman in his arms. She wasn't supposed to wiggle her way into his heart so easily. Now he fully understood what had happened to Donovan.

He glanced down at Brittany. The sound of her crying tore at his heart. But he was letting her get it all out—all the pain, heartache, heartbreak, loneliness, the feeling of belonging to no one. And as she cried he gently rubbed her back, held her in his arms and whispered over and over again that everything would be okay.

He doubted when it was over she would remember even half the stuff she'd told him just now, but he would never forget it. She thought she'd never liked sex? A part of him inwardly smiled knowing she'd certainly enjoyed it last night. Was that what last night had been about? Testing the waters to see if perhaps, considering all the sexual chemistry between them, she could possibly enjoy it with him?

And what was all that about her fingers and legs? Was that why she hadn't gotten adopted as a baby? Most people wanted newborns instead of an older child, and for her not to have gotten adopted meant that someone thought something was wrong with her. So, she'd had a couple of crooked fingers and weak legs, big damn deal. Was that a good reason not to take a baby into your home and love it? And he would love to be in the same room as this Ponder guy about now. He'd put both his feet up the man's rear end.

Pulling in a deep breath, he continued to rock her and kept whispering that everything would be okay.

Earlier that afternoon he'd begun getting concerned when she hadn't returned, and when she hadn't answered her cell phone, concern turned to worry. A first for him over a woman.

All he could think was that she was alone in a house on a secluded road. He'd driven like a maniac to get here. And now that he was here with her, there was no need to question why his heart was filled with so much love for her.

Damn.

And with that realization he could only shake his head. No need to ask how it happened, where it happened or when it happened. Those logistics really didn't matter. All that mattered was that he had fallen hopelessly in love with Brittany Thrasher. Especially when it had been just yesterday he'd assured himself his fascination with her was bound to wear off. Today he realized he had no intentions of letting her go. Ever.

When she finally pulled her face from his chest and tried wiping away any traces of tears, he asked softly, "Where's your cell phone, sweetheart? I tried calling you a hundred times."

She didn't look up at him, pretending interest in the buttons of his shirt. She was probably trying to recall just how much she'd told him. No doubt she figured she'd given him too much information.

"It's in my purse on top of the washing machine. I guess I didn't hear it ring."

"Okay, we'll grab it on our way out." He then swept her into his arms. At her gasp of surprise he looked down at her and said, "And before you ask, I'm taking you home."

She really didn't have a clue just how much he meant it.

"You are mine," a raspy voice whispered as Brittany felt her clothes being removed from her body. She couldn't stay awake. She felt so sleepy.

She recalled Galen bringing her back here and leaving her car at her mother's place. The drive over here was a blur, but she did remember him carrying her into the house and then up the stairs to his bedroom.

She had the faintest memory of him giving her a glass of wine to drink, but only because the sweet taste of fermented grape was still on her tongue. And now Galen was whispering to her, letting her know he was removing her clothes and getting her ready for bed. That only made her want to cry even more because no one had ever really taken care of her. But tonight he was.

"Hold up your arms, Brittany, so I can slip the T-shirt on you."

Like a child, she did what she was told, because all she wanted to do was sleep. And she shivered when she felt the cotton material sliding over her head and past her shoulders to hardly cover her thighs.

Through barely opened eyes, she watched as he tossed the covers back and then, reaching his hand out to her, she took it and slid beneath the covers. When he tucked her in, a tear fell from her eye. No one had ever tucked her into bed before.

"You're going to read me a story?" she asked, trying to tease but barely getting the words out. She had a feeling she'd taken too many sips of wine.

"Do you want me to?" he asked, and she felt his callused fingertips brush across her cheek. So gentle.

"Yes, but nothing sad."

She felt the bed dip and knew he'd slid in bed beside

her, fully clothed, to gather her into his arms. She inhaled his scent and took comfort in his nearness.

"This story has a happy ending," he whispered close to her ear.

"All right."

"There once was a man name Drew, who had so many women he didn't know what to do. And he thought he was happy until one day he saw this girl named Eden, and figured he would make her another one of his women. But he soon realized Eden was special. She couldn't be like his other women. Because this girl had done something the others couldn't do. She had captured his heart. And then he and Eden got married and lived happily ever after."

She snuggled closer to him and his warmth. "Hmm, nice." And then she drifted off to sleep.

Chapter 16

Brittany opened her eyes and stared up at the gray clouds in the sky. It was supposed to rain today, wasn't it? She closed her eyes, not sure what day it was. Sunday, she believed.

Parts of yesterday floated through her memory. She remembered going to her house and washing the bed linens and then finding her mother's journal.

She opened her eyes. The journal. She recalled reading the journal and the parts that had made her cry. And she remembered Galen showing up and holding her while she cried and bringing her back here.

Brittany threw back the covers and glanced down at herself. She was wearing one of his T-shirts. The details of last night were sketchy, but she did recall him undressing her and tucking her into bed. He'd even told her some story, although she couldn't exactly remember it. Hopefully, it would all come back later.

She eased out of bed and stretched. She needed to shower, put on some clothes and go apologize to Galen for her actions yesterday. It was not good manners for a woman to get all emotional on a man.

As she headed toward the bathroom, she promised herself that she would make it up to him.

"So, Galen, where's your houseguest?"

Galen stared across the table at Jonas. This brother had asked the very question the other four were wondering but hadn't the nerve to inquire about. Galen was no fool. He'd known the moment he had opened the door to them that they had visited for a reason. He couldn't recall the last time they'd dropped by bringing him breakfast.

"Brittany's upstairs," he said as he continued eating.

"Nice name," Gannon interjected.

Galen nodded. "She's a nice girl."

"Classify nice."

That had come from Tyson. Eli, he noticed, wasn't saying anything. He was just looking, listening and eating. "She's not anyone I'd typically mess around with."

"Then why are you?" Mercury asked.

Galen smiled. "Because I like her." He thought about what he'd just said and decided these five men deserved his honesty, even though what he was about to say would stun them. "In fact, I'm in love with her."

Their reaction was comical at best. Only Eli had managed to keep a straight face—one of those "I told you so" expressions. The others looked shocked.

"What do you mean you love her? The way Drew loves Eden or the way Colfax loves Velvet?" Mercury asked.

Everyone was familiar with Mercury's friend Jaye Colfax. He claimed he was in love with Velvet Spencer; however, he wasn't in love with the woman, just the sex because it was off the chain.

"It's like Drew and Eden."

That confession was like a missile going off in his kitchen, and with it came a blast. Colorful expletives were discharged in different languages because he and all of his brothers spoke several foreign languages. In fact, maybe that was a good thing considering Brittany was upstairs. He hadn't heard her moving around, but that didn't mean she hadn't awakened. The last thing she needed to hear was the Steele brothers discussing her.

"Let's speak German," Galen suggested.

English or German, what his brothers were saying was scorching his ears. He was being called everything but a child of God. Now he knew how Donovan felt, because Galen had been one of the first to read his cousin the riot act, as if falling in love was something he could have avoided.

When he felt they'd pretty much gotten everything

off their chests, and probably every filthy word they could think of out of their mouths, he stood and said in German, "Okay, you've all had your say, now get over it."

It wasn't just what he said, but the tone he used that made his kitchen suddenly get quiet. Five pairs of green eyes stared at him. And then he said, "What happens to me has no bearing on the five of you."

He knew it was a lie even as he said it. Eden Tyson Steele wouldn't see it that way. She would think one down and five more to go.

"And you truly love her? This woman you met...less than a week ago?" Jonas asked, looking at him like he ought to have his head examined.

"We didn't just meet. I met her in New York six months ago."

"Hey, wait a minute," Gannon said, as if something had just clicked inside his head. "Is she the one who got away?"

Galen couldn't help but smile. Gannon had a tendency to remember everything. "Yes, she's the one, which is why I don't plan on letting her get away again."

"So when is the wedding?" Jonas asked. "If I'm going to be in a wedding, I need to know when. My schedule is pretty crazy for the next few months."

Galen shrugged. "Don't know because she hasn't a clue how I feel. And chances are she might not return the feelings."

His brothers looked aghast at such a possibility. After all, Galen was a Steele and all women loved the Steeles.

"So you're going to have to work on her? Convince her you're worthy of her affections?" Tyson asked, as if the thought of Galen doing such a thing was downright shameful.

"Yes, and I intend to win her over."

"And if you don't?"

An assured and confident smile touched his lips. "I will."

Brittany was halfway down the stairs when she heard the sound of male voices…and they were speaking in a different language. German, she believed, but wasn't sure. The only other language she spoke was Spanish. Why would they be doing such a thing? She stopped walking, wondering if she should interrupt.

She shrugged. A few days ago when she'd asked about meeting his brothers, Galen had said they'd come around sooner or later, when word got out about her. They were here, so evidently word was out and she might as well get it over with and make an appearance.

She walked into the kitchen. "Good morning."

The room went silent and six pairs of eyes turned to her. Her gaze immediately latched onto Galen's as the other men just stared at her. The one thing she did notice was that they appeared to be sextuplets. All six had the same height and build and those Smokey Robinson eyes. And all were handsome as sin.

Galen walked over to her and she felt a semblance of relief because his brothers just continued to eye her up and down. She was glad she looked pretty decent in her knit top and skirt.

"Okay, guys, I want you to meet Brittany Thrasher," Galen said, wrapping one arm around her waist. "Brittany, from left to right, that's Tyson, Eli, Jonas, Mercury and Gannon."

She smiled warmly, then said, "Nice meeting all of you."

But the men didn't reply. They just continued to gawk. "It's not polite to stare."

Simultaneously, their faces broke into smiles and Brittany knew Nikki's warnings about these brothers were true. They were Phoenix's most eligible bachelors, heartbreakers to the core. Even the one standing close by her side.

"Sorry. Please forgive our manners," the one introduced as Tyson said. "Your beauty has left us speechless."

Yeah, right, she thought to herself. This one, Dr. Tyson Steele, was the epitome of suave and sophisticated, exuding an aura of self-assurance and confidence. Instead of saying what she really thought about his compliment, though, she decided to accept it graciously. "Thank you."

"My brothers brought breakfast. Please join us," Galen invited.

She shook her head. "That's okay. I didn't mean to interrupt."

"And you didn't," Eli said. "Please join us. We insist."

Her gaze lit on the man who looked like he could easily grace the cover of *GQ*. In fact they all did, including Galen. She allowed herself a moment to size up the brothers the same way they were doing with her. They were probably trying to figure things out between her and their brother. Evidently, Galen hadn't told them much and now they probably wanted to pump information out of her.

She'd never had siblings, so she didn't know how they operated collectively. But she had a feeling those Steeles were rather unique when it came to looking out for each other. She wondered if they saw her as a threat to Galen for some reason.

Deciding to go along with the invitation, she said, "Thanks. I'd love to join you for breakfast."

She glanced up at Galen. His arms were still around her waist, but he had an odd look on his face. Had he expected her to turn down his invitation? Sometimes she could read him and sometimes she could not.

This was one of those times.

Galen leaned back in his chair watching Brittany. She conversed and joked easily with his brothers and they had definitely warmed up to her. Over breakfast she had told them about her business and in kind, they told her about theirs. That unfortunately extended their stay. He was about to suggest they think about leaving when Jonas remembered their golf game at noon, and the five reluctantly left.

"I like your brothers," Brittany said when Galen

returned after walking them to the door with strict orders not to come back anytime soon.

"They're okay." He had sat there and watched her interactions with his siblings, thinking of just how well she would fit in with his family. His parents would adore her; especially his mother. Brittany said she'd never had a family before; well, she had one now. His brothers didn't take to people easily. They were usually guarded and reserved. But they had taken to her.

"Did you sleep well last night?" he asked, walking over to her.

He saw the blush that stained her cheeks when she said, "Yes. I didn't mean to be so much trouble. I see you got me ready for bed and tucked me in."

And I told you a story you probably don't remember, he thought. "You weren't any trouble. I didn't mind taking care of you."

"But you shouldn't have had to. That wasn't part of our agreement, Galen."

Damn the agreement, he wanted to say. Instead he said, "So what are your plans today? We left your car at the house. Do you want to go back and get it now or do you want to wait until later?"

"I'll wait until later, if you don't mind. Do you usually work on your video games on Sunday, as well?"

"It depends on what I have to do to it. Sniper is relatively finished except for a few components. Would you like to see it?"

He could tell by her expression she was surprised he'd asked. "Can I?"

"Sure. Come on."

She followed him to the door that led to his garage. He opened it and then held it for her to precede him through it and down the steps. "Is this a garage or a dungeon?" she threw over her shoulder to ask.

He laughed as he closed the door and followed her downstairs. "In a way it's both. My house is built on a high peak, but the driveway is on a slope, which means you have to drive down to the garage. It's a six-car garage."

"You have that many cars?"

He chuckled. "Not yet, but I'm working on it. I collect vintage cars, specifically muscle cars," he said when they reached the bottom.

She glanced over at him. "What's a muscle car?"

"It's a high-performance automobile that was manufactured in the late sixties and early seventies. I own three now and I'm always looking to add more to my collection."

She glanced around. "This is a huge area and I've never seen a garage floor that's tiled, and with such nice stone pavers."

He smiled. "Thanks. Come on. I'll show you my cars and then I'll let you watch me work with Sniper."

Brittany followed Galen and admired the vintage cars he had in his collection. They were beautiful, all three of them—a 1967 Camaro, a 1969 GTO and a 1968 Road Runner. They went along with his everyday cars, the late-model SUV, Corvette and Mercedes sedan.

"Where did you get your interest in muscle cars?"

she asked, admiring the sleek design and craftsmanship of each vehicle. She didn't know a lot about cars, but she could tell these were in great shape. A collector's dream.

"My father. He has his own collection," he explained as he led her over to his work area.

She couldn't believe how spacious his work space was, and how neat and organized. She could see why he preferred working in his garage instead of an off-site office or warehouse. Everything was at his fingertips here.

He offered her the seat next to his and then proceeded to explain how the video game would work and what he needed to do to get it ready for the Video Game Expo in the spring. She could hear the excitement in his voice when he told her about it. She was touched that he was sharing his work with her. He hadn't invited her in here before and she wondered why he was doing so now. Still, it felt good knowing he had allowed her into his private space.

Brittany scooted her chair closer as he talked her through the assembly of one of the components of the game. Everything was being designed on a huge computer screen in front of him. She was amazed at how much graphic art expertise went into the creation of a game, as well as the game engine. The more she watched, the more she admired his skill, proficiency and imagination.

She glanced over at him. His face was set with determination and concentration. But he was her focal point as she studied him, scanned his features with the intensity of a woman who wanted a man.

She liked watching his hands move and remembered those same hands moving over her as his fingertips caressed the curve of her breasts, cupped her backside or slid between her thighs. A rush of heat hit her in the chest as her body responded to the memories. She let out a slow breath.

"Getting bored?" he asked, glancing over at her.

"No, not at all. I enjoy looking at you work." *And I enjoy looking at you.*

She watched him save whatever program he'd been working on and then turn to her. Galen had a way of looking at her that left her breathless, made her hot. Made the area between her legs tingle.

"You ever make out in the backseat of a car?"

She clamped her mouth shut to keep it from dropping open. Was she really supposed to answer that? Evidently, because he seemed to be waiting on her response. "No."

"You want to try it?" There was that arrogant smile on his face. The one she both loved and detested.

"Before you answer, let me tell you how it will work," he said, leaning closer so that his heated breath came into contact with her skin. "The backseat of the car will be the ending point. We will actually start here in my work space. I want to take you all over it."

His words sent a surge of anticipation through her. Adrenaline pumped through her bloodstream; visual imagery danced in her head. "I'll start off by licking you all over and then going inside you so deep, you won't know where your body ends and mine begins."

He reached out and with the tip of his finger he caressed her arm. She could feel the goose bumps forming there. "And after we make love over in this area a few times…"

A few times? Mercy.

"Then we'll move to the cars. You can take your pick."

Boy, was he generous. In more ways than one. His fingers had moved from her arm and had dropped to her thigh and were now slowly sliding beneath her skirt. One spot he touched made her quiver inside. And she was convinced her panties were getting wet.

"So, Brittany Thrasher, what do you say?"

She couldn't say anything. She wasn't capable of speech. As an intense ache spread all over her body, she reached up and wrapped her arms around his neck. She decided to let her actions show him what she couldn't put into words.

Chapter 17

Galen didn't have a problem with Brittany taking the initiative with this kiss after he'd planted a few sensuous seeds in her mind. He would use any tactic he thought would work. He was determined to bind her to him and they might as well start here, because they did enjoy making love.

And today he intended for there to be plenty of foreplay. When it was all said and done, Brittany would know without a doubt that she was his. Permanently and irrevocably.

While her tongue tangled with his, she began kneading the muscles in his shoulders, heating his blood to flash point. He pulled her out of her chair and into his lap, scooting his own chair back from the table so that her body was practically draped over his.

And then he took over the kiss and decided to seduce her Galen Steele–style. The exploration of her mouth was intense and he intended for his tongue to leave a mark wherever it went. He was on the verge of getting intoxicated just with a kiss and a touch. Then he slid his fingers into her womanly folds, and her groan sent spirals of intense longing right to his crotch, making his erection press hard against the zipper of his jeans.

With her in his arms he stood and stripped her naked in record time, for desire consumed him in a way it never had before. When he was done with hers, he removed his own clothes and noticed her staring down at his erection.

"You want it, Brittany?"

She glanced up at him. "Yes, I want it."

"Then take it."

He didn't have to say the words twice. She eased down in front of him.

"I've never done this before," she said, looking up at him, "but I want so much to do it for you."

He smiled down at her. "Practice makes perfect."

"And if you don't like it?"

"I'm going to like it. Trust me."

She held his gaze for a moment and then said in a soft voice, "I do trust you, Galen."

And then she dipped her head and took him into the warmth of her mouth. Every part of his body, every cell and molecule, quivered in response. Her hand gripped him while her mouth drove him crazy. Using her tongue she covered every inch of him, from the tip all the way to the base.

He reached out and tightened his hand in her hair and let out a deep guttural groan. Had she actually thought he wouldn't like this? How could he not like the feel of her hot tongue gliding over him, and then pulling him inside the sweet recesses of her mouth? When he felt a deep throbbing about to erupt, he quickly pulled her up and swept her into his arms and placed her on his work desk, spreading her legs in the process.

He sheathed himself with a condom and made good his threat to lick her all over. With erotic caresses his tongue covered every inch of her, intent on giving her the pleasures she thought she could never enjoy. And he didn't let up until he had her on the verge of a climax. But then he didn't really let up; he delved in deeper, using his tongue to deliver powerful strokes. She moaned and writhed beneath his mouth.

And then she screamed, shuddered uncontrollably and clutched the sides of his head as the intense sensations erupted inside her. Sensations Galen felt in his mouth. He hadn't been prepared for a woman like her. He hadn't been prepared to fall in love with her.

But he had.

When he pulled his mouth away while licking his lips, he leaned forward and whispered in her ear, "Now we make out in my car."

Galen knew for the rest of the day he would continue to assault her mind with desire and fill her body with pleasure. He couldn't imagine ever being inside any other woman but her for the rest of his days.

And as he picked her up into his arms and carried her toward his 1969 GTO, he knew that sex between them would never be enough. But he intended to make it a good start.

Brittany stepped out of the shower and caught her reflection in the vanity mirror and couldn't help but smile. For someone who'd started out the week with hidden pleasures, Galen had done a pretty good job of uncovering them.

Her smile slowly faded when she remembered they had only two more days and then their week together would end. She thought of her mother's home as hers, and had even gone so far as to order repairs to those areas that needed it. And she would be interviewing a painter later today after having lunch with Nikki.

She would leave Saturday morning to fly back to Tampa with plans to return to Phoenix in a week's time. She had finished reading all of her mother's entries in the journal and continued to feel the love her mother had for her. She'd thought about expanding the house and using it to open a home base for Etiquette Matters. She had discussed the idea with Galen, who thought it was a good one.

The only problem she saw—and it was her problem— was how she would handle it when she returned to Phoenix and ran into him with another woman. She knew they didn't have any hold on each other; they weren't even dating. Their agreement was for her to live with him for a week and she was only two days short of fulfilling her terms. But she knew leaving here would be the hardest thing she'd ever had to do.

Because she'd fallen in love with him.

Every time he touched her, made love to her, she fell deeper and deeper in love with him. Emotions washed over her and they were emotions she had no right to feel where Galen Steele was concerned. He hadn't made any promises, hadn't alluded to the possibility that he felt anything for her. To a man like him, sex was sex. When their affair ended, his affair with another woman would begin. Her heart ached at the thought, but she knew it to be true. She had fallen in love with him, but he hadn't fallen in love with her.

She pulled in a deep breath. That was the story of her life. None of the couples wanting to adopt a child had found her worthy, either. But deep down she believed she had a lot to offer a man. That man just wasn't Galen.

She lifted her chin as she proceeded to rub lotion on her body. As far as she was concerned it was his loss and not hers.

"Have you told Brittany how you feel?"

Galen glanced up at Eli. He had stopped by his brother's office to sign papers for SID. "No, I haven't told her."

One of Eli's brows rose. "What the hell are you waiting for?"

Galen leaned back in his chair, thinking Eli's question

was a good one. The only excuse he could come up with was that the last few days with Brittany had been perfect and he hadn't wanted to do anything to mess them up. He had no idea how she would react to such an admission on his part, especially because she seemed content with how things were now.

In the mornings she was over at her place taking care of her mother's belongings while he worked on perfecting Sniper. Then in the afternoon she would arrive home and they'd spend time together. One afternoon they'd gone hiking, another time they'd shared his hot tub, and still another day he'd given her lessons on how to properly use a bow and arrow. He enjoyed having her in his space and spending time with her.

And at night he enjoyed sleeping with her. Making love to her under the moon or the stars overhead. She was so responsive that they had to be the most intense lovemaking sessions of his life. Even the breathless aftermath made him shiver inside just thinking about it.

He also enjoyed waking up with her wrapped in his arms every morning, and making love to her before either of them started their day. And they would talk. She trusted him enough to share her secret with him about Mr. Ponder and why making love to Galen had been a crucial step to overcoming her inability to enjoy sex.

He was well aware that Brittany assumed that in two days she would be leaving, walking out of his life, and he hadn't a clue how to break it to her that that was not how things were going to be.

"Galen?"

He glanced up to find Eli staring at him. "What?"

"When are you going to tell Brittany how you feel about her? Doesn't she leave in a couple of days?"

"Yes, but she'll be back."

"Back to Phoenix but not to your place. She thinks when she leaves here Saturday morning what's between the two of you will be over."

Galen pulled in a deep breath, not surprised Eli knew as much as he did. Brittany had sought him out to handle a couple of legal issues regarding her house. She was trying to get the area rezoned to open the headquarters for Etiquette Matters.

"Nothing between us will be over. I love her," Galen said.

"Then maybe you ought to tell her that. She needs to know she's worthy of being loved."

Galen ran his hand down his face. Over the last few days, even though he'd warned them to stay away, his brothers had revisited anyway and had grown attached to Brittany. They were now her champions and wanted to make sure he would do the right thing by her, although he'd told them from day one what his feelings had been.

"She's never been part of a family and I want so much for her to feel a part of ours."

"Then tomorrow night will be perfect. Thursday-night dinner at Mom's."

Galen's head jerked up. Damn, why hadn't he thought of that? Eli was right. Galen had never brought a woman home to meet his mother before. None of them had. She would have to know the importance of that, wouldn't she? And if she didn't, he would explain things to her.

"That's a good idea."

Eli grinned. "Thank you."

Galen eyed his brother suspiciously. "And just what's in it for you?"

Eli's features broke into a serious expression when he said, "Your happiness."

Galen held his brother's gaze and then nodded. He and his brothers might have inherited Drew's horny genes, but they'd also inherited Eden's caring genes, as well.

"Okay, there's no way after tomorrow night Brittany won't know how I feel."

Once Galen had left his brother's office and slid behind the steering wheel of his car, he pulled out his cell phone and punched in a few numbers.

A feminine voice picked up on the second ring. "Hello."

"Mom, this is Galen. And I'm keeping my promise that you'd be one of the first to know." He couldn't help but smile. His brothers had been the first to know, but there was no reason to tell Eden Steele that.

"Know what?"

"There's a woman I'm interested in." He shook his head and decided to go for broke. "I'm in love with her and I'd like to bring her to dinner tomorrow night."

Chapter 18

Brittany checked her lipstick again before putting the small mirror back in her purse. She then glanced over at Galen as he drove to his parents' home for dinner. "Are you sure I look okay?"

Without taking his eyes off the road, he said, "You look great. I love that outfit, by the way."

She smiled. "Thanks. Nikki and I went shopping yesterday and I bought it then." She had introduced him to Nikki a few days ago. She had been helping her with packing up her mother's things. She felt so very blessed having her best friend back in her life.

"So this is a weekly event for you and your brothers with your parents?" she asked.

"Yes. Just for our family. No outsiders."

Brittany frowned. Then why had she gotten invited?

She shrugged. Evidently Galen felt he would lack manners if he were to not include his houseguest. She felt bad knowing the only reason she'd been invited was because he'd felt compelled to bring her.

"What time do you fly out Saturday morning to return to Tampa?" he asked her.

"Eight." She couldn't help wondering if the reason he was asking was because he was eager for her to leave. Her heart ached at the thought.

"Well, here we are."

Brittany glanced through the window and saw the huge house whose exterior was beautifully decorated for the holidays. It was twice the size of Galen's home. "And this is the house you lived in as a child?" she couldn't help asking.

"Yes. We moved in here when I was in the first grade. My parents knew they wanted a lot of children and went ahead and purchased a house that could accommodate a large family."

Brittany nodded, thinking that made perfect sense.

Galen brought the car to a stop among several others and she said, "Looks like your brothers are here already."

"Yes, it looks that way."

She felt relieved. Over the last few days she'd gotten to know Galen's brothers and truly liked them. She wouldn't feel so out of place with them around. She could just imagine what Galen's mother was going to think when she walked in with him.

"Ready?" Galen asked, glancing over at her.

She released a deep breath and said, "Yes, I'm ready."

Brittany took a sip of her wine thinking it odd that Galen's parents hadn't asked how they met or how long they'd known each other. It seemed the moment she and Galen had walked in and all eyes turned to them, she'd felt a strange sort of connection to his mother. It was as if beneath all her outer beauty was a heart of gold. Someone beautiful on the inside as well as the outside. And Eden Tyson Steele was beautiful. She didn't look as if she should be the mother of six sons. The woman didn't look a day over forty, if that. And it was plain to see her husband simply adored her.

It was also plain to see that although Galen and his brothers had their mother's eyes, the rest of their features belonged to Drew Steele. The man was tall, dark and definitely handsome, and Brittany could just imagine him being a devilish rogue in his day, capturing the hearts of many women but giving his heart to only one.

She'd asked Galen how his parents had met and he'd said his father owned a trucking company and was doing a run one night from Phoenix to California, filling in for a sick driver, when he came across Eden, who'd stowed away in the back of his truck at a truck stop, in an attempt to get away from an overbearing agent.

The moment Brittany had walked in with Galen, Eden had given her a smile that Brittany felt was truly genuine and the woman seemed pleased that Galen had brought her to dinner with him. Galen's father was kind as well, and it was quite obvious that he loved and respected his sons and were proud of the men they'd become.

Brittany had never been around such a close-knit family.

"You okay?"

She glanced up at Galen and smiled. "Yes, I'm fine."

He'd rarely left her side and when and if he had, one or all of his brothers had been right there. Except for the time his mother asked if she wanted to see how she had personally decorated the courtyard for the holidays.

Brittany had figured the woman had wanted to get her alone to grill her about her life and discovered that had not been the case. They had talked about fashion, movies and things women talk about when they get together. Brittany found herself talking comfortably, and had told Eden about the home she'd inherited from her birth mother. She had found it so easy to talk to Galen's mother and a part of her wished things were different between her and Galen. Eden would be the type of mother-in-law any woman would want to have. But she knew she would never be hers because she and Galen didn't have that sort of relationship. For some strange reason, though, Brittany had a feeling his family thought otherwise.

"So what do you think of my parents?" he leaned close and asked her.

"I think you are blessed to have them. They are super."

"Yes, they are," he agreed. "And what do you think of my mother's courtyard?"

Brittany grinned. "If I wasn't in the holiday spirit before arriving here, I would definitely be now."

Galen threw his head back and laughed, and Brittany couldn't help herself when she joined in with him. His mother's courtyard looked like a Christmas wonderland. Beautiful as well as festive.

"Christmas is her favorite holiday," he said, placing an arm around her shoulders and bringing her closer to his side.

She lifted her glass to her lips and smiled before taking a sip of her wine. "I can tell."

It didn't take a rocket scientist to see his parents were taken with Brittany, Galen thought. From the moment she walked into their home, Drew and Eden had begun treating her like the daughter they'd never had. Galen could tell that at first Brittany was overwhelmed, didn't know what to make of such an overflow of love and kindness, but then he figured she assumed that's just the way his parents were.

Not really.

He would be the first to admit his parents were good people, but even he had noticed how solicitous they were toward her. And his brothers were no exception. They flocked around her like the caring brothers they would become once they married. He had thought of that word a lot lately and he knew he truly wanted to marry Brittany. He couldn't imagine his life without her.

They needed to talk, he knew, and he'd start that conversation in earnest when they returned to his place.

Now he crossed the room to where Brittany stood talking to his parents and brothers.

"Time to go, sweetheart," he said softly.

She smiled over at him. "All right." She then turned to his parents. "Thanks so much for having me here tonight."

Eden beamed. "And we look forward to you coming back." She then shifted her gaze to her oldest son. "You will bring her back, Galen, won't you?"

Galen grinned. "Yes, whenever she's in town. If I come, she'll be with me."

"Wonderful!"

Galen noticed on the way back home that Brittany seemed awfully quiet. He knew for sure something was bothering her when they arrived back at his place and he saw her lips quivering. She was mad about something. What? He found out the moment he closed the door behind them.

"How could you do that, Galen?" she asked angrily. "How could you let your parents assume I meant something to you and I'd be back to have dinner with them again when you don't want me? Do you know how that made me feel?"

Yes, Galen thought, leaning back against the door. He knew precisely how she felt. She had gone through life assuming no one wanted her. In her eyes, she had been the flawed baby no one wanted to adopt. Not worthy of anyone's love. Well, he had news for her and he might as well set her straight right now and not while making love to her later tonight as he'd planned.

He moved away from the door and crossed the distance separating them. When he came to a stop in front of her, he saw the tears she was trying hard to hold back and promised himself that he would never let her shed a single tear for thinking no one wanted her.

"It should have made you feel loved, Brittany, because you are. My parents treated you the way they did tonight because they knew what you evidently don't. Granted, I've never said the words, but I'd thought my actions spoke loud and clear. I love you."

He could tell she didn't get it for a moment because she just stood there and stared at him. And then she spoke. "What did you say?"

He had no trouble repeating it. "I said I love you. I love you so much I ache. I believe I fell in love with you that day in New York when you saw me at my worst. And when I saw you again here in Phoenix, I knew I would do whatever it took to have you with me, even concocting a plan to bid on the house you wanted just so you'd stay a week here with me. Of course I didn't think you would go for it, but I wanted you to have the house anyway. In fact, when you get back to Tampa you'll have the packet Eli sent giving you the house free and clear *before* you decided to take my offer."

Brittany blinked. "But, if that was the case, then why did you still make me think I had to stay here for a week?"

He gave her an arrogant smile. "Because I wanted you in my bed. I'm a Steele."

She just stood there and stared at him for a long

moment and then a smile trembled on her lips. "Your conceit is showing again," she pointed out.

"Sorry."

"I'm not. I love you just the way you are. And I do love you, Galen. I was so afraid you couldn't love me."

Another smile touched his lips, this one filled with care, concern and sincerity. "You are an easy person to love, Brittany. If there is any way I could redo your childhood, I would. But I think you're the person that you are because of it and the challenges you had to face," he said, reaching out and caressing her cheek with his thumb.

"But for the rest of your days, I will make up for all the love you didn't get. I will love you and honor you."

"Oh, Galen." Tears she couldn't hold back streamed down her face.

It was then that Galen swept her off her feet and into his arms to carry her up the stairs. "I told my brothers how I felt about you that day they met you and advised my parents yesterday. Tonight they treated you just as they should have—as a person who will soon become an official member of our family."

He looked down at her and paused on the stair. "Will you marry me?"

Brittany smiled up at him. "Yes! Yes, I will marry you."

Galen grinned as he continued walking up the stairs to his bedroom. "Just so you'll know, I'm having your ring specially designed by Zion."

Brittany's mouth dropped open. "I'm getting a ring by Zion?"

Galen threw his head back and laughed when he placed her on the bed. "Yes." He knew any jewelry by Zion was the rave because Zion was the First Lady's personal jeweler.

She beamed. "I feel special."

"Always keep that thought, because you are."

Galen glanced down at the woman he had placed on his bed. His soul mate. The woman he would love forever. The thought nearly overwhelmed him. "And just so you'll know, I've cleared my work schedule. I'm going with you back to Tampa."

Surprise lit her face. "You are?"

"Yes. I don't intend to let you out of my sight." He dipped his knee on the bed. "Now come here." When she lifted a brow, he added, "Please."

Brittany chuckled as she moved toward Galen and when he wrapped her in his arms and kissed her, she felt completely loved by the one man who had discovered all her hidden pleasures. "How could things be this way for us this soon?"

He understood her question and had a good reason for what probably seemed like madness. "My mother has always warned her sons that we're like our father in a lot of ways," he said. "We're known to be skirt chasers until we meet the one woman who will claim our hearts. You are that woman for me, Brittany. I realized just how empty my life has been until this week while you were here with me. I love you."

She fought back tears in her eyes when she said, "And I love you, too."

And then Galen kissed her and she knew a lot of people would think their affair had been rather short, but she knew it had been just like it was meant to be. Now they would embark upon a life together filled with romance and passion.

Epilogue

Four months later

Galen glanced around the room at all the Steeles in attendance. The last time they'd all gotten together had been at Donovan's wedding in New York. Now they'd all assembled here in Phoenix to watch the first of Drew's boys take the plunge. And very happily, he might add.

Nikki had been Brittany's bridesmaid and his father had been his best man. They'd wanted it simple and decided to have a wedding on the grounds of the home Brittany's mother had left her. Brittany felt her mother's presence there and wanted to start their life off surrounded by love.

"So, what were the nasty things you said to me when

I told you I was getting married?" his cousin Donovan said, pulling him out of his reverie.

Galen smiled. "Okay, that was before I knew better. Before I understood the power of love." He glanced over to where Brittany stood with his mother and his heart expanded twice the size.

"You have a beautiful bride and I wish the two of you happiness always."

"Thanks, Donovan."

Deciding his mother had taken up enough of his wife's time, Galen crossed the room and when Brittany glanced up and saw him, she smiled. She had been a beautiful bride and looked absolutely radiant. And when he opened his arms, she stepped into his embrace. They would be leaving later that day to fly to London where they would catch a ship for a twelve-day Mediterranean cruise.

"I love you, Mrs. Steele," he whispered, holding her tight in his arms.

She smiled up at him. "And I love you."

Over his shoulders he saw his mother eyeing his brothers, who seemed oblivious of her perusal. Galen knew exactly how their mother's mind worked. She was thinking, "One down, five to go."

His brothers would deal with Eden Steele as they saw fit. Galen knew he would have his hands full with the beautiful, sexy woman in his arms. She would continue to teach him manners and he intended to make sure her pleasures were never hidden again.

"Are you ready for your wedding gift now, Galen?"

He arched a brow. "I have another one?" A couple of days ago she had given him a new digital camera. And she'd given him a book on manners. He had given her a gold bracelet with the inscription "Galen's Lady." And he'd given her a toy yellow cab to replace the one he'd taken from her that day in New York.

"Yes, you have another one. I'm not going to blindfold you but you must promise to close your eyes and keep them closed until I say you can open them."

"All right."

He closed his eyes and felt himself being led no telling where, and after a few minutes, Brittany instructed, "You can open them now, Galen."

He did and sucked in a quick breath when he saw the car he'd wanted, the 1969 Chevelle, parked only a few feet away from where he stood. He couldn't believe it. It looked beautiful, but then when he glanced over at Brittany, he knew she was the most beautiful thing in his life.

"But how?" he asked, barely able to get the words out past his excitement.

She smiled. "After you confessed to eavesdropping on my and Nikki's conversation that day, I felt bad that you missed out on the chance to bid for this car because of me, so I gave your brothers the job of locating it for me. Luckily, they did. I hope you like it."

"Oh, sweetheart, I love it, but not as much as I love you." He pulled her into his arms intent on showing her how much. He took her mouth in a lingering kiss, not caring if his brothers or any of the other wedding guests could see them.

She was his and he was hers. Forever.

* * * * *

REQUEST YOUR FREE BOOKS!

2 FREE NOVELS
PLUS 2 FREE GIFTS!

KIMANI™ ROMANCE

Love's ultimate destination!

YES! Please send me 2 FREE Kimani™ Romance novels and my 2 FREE gifts (gifts are worth about $10). After receiving them, if I don't wish to receive any more books, I can return the shipping statement marked "cancel." If I don't cancel, I will receive 4 brand-new novels every month and be billed just $4.69 per book in the U.S. or $5.24 per book in Canada. That's a saving of over 20% off the cover price. It's quite a bargain! Shipping and handling is just 50¢ per book.* I understand that accepting the 2 free books and gifts places me under no obligation to buy anything. I can always return a shipment and cancel at any time. Even if I never buy another book from Kimani Press, the two free books and gifts are mine to keep forever.

168/368 XDN E7PZ

Name	(PLEASE PRINT)
Address	Apt. #
City	State/Prov.	Zip/Postal Code

Signature (if under 18, a parent or guardian must sign)

Mail to **The Reader Service:**
IN U.S.A.: P.O. Box 1867, Buffalo, NY 14240-1867
IN CANADA: P.O. Box 609, Fort Erie, Ontario L2A 5X3

Not valid for current subscribers to Kimani Romance books.

Want to try two free books from another line?
Call 1-800-873-8635 or visit www.morefreebooks.com.

* Terms and prices subject to change without notice. Prices do not include applicable taxes. N.Y. residents add applicable sales tax. Canadian residents will be charged applicable provincial taxes and GST. Offer not valid in Quebec. This offer is limited to one order per household. All orders subject to approval. Credit or debit balances in a customer's account(s) may be offset by any other outstanding balance owed by or to the customer. Please allow 4 to 6 weeks for delivery. Offer available while quantities last.

Your Privacy: Kimani Press is committed to protecting your privacy. Our Privacy Policy is available online at www.eHarlequin.com or upon request from the Reader Service. From time to time we make our lists of customers available to reputable third parties who may have a product or service of interest to you. If you would prefer we not share your name and address, please check here. ☐

Help us get it right—We strive for accurate, respectful and relevant communications. To clarify or modify your communication preferences, visit us at www.ReaderService.com/consumerschoice.

KROM10R

L🌑VE IN THE LIMELIGHT

Fantasy, Fame and Fortune...Hollywood-Style!

Book #1

By *New York Times* and *USA TODAY*
Bestselling Author Brenda Jackson

STAR OF HIS HEART

August 2010

Book #2

By A.C. Arthur

SING YOUR PLEASURE

September 2010

Book #3

By Ann Christopher

SEDUCED ON THE RED CARPET

October 2010

Book #4

By *Essence* Bestselling Author Adrianne Byrd

LOVERS PREMIERE

November 2010

Set in Hollywood's entertainment industry,
two unstoppable sisters and their two friends
find romance, glamour and dreams-come-true.

KIMANI™
ROMANCE

www.kimanipress.com
www.myspace.com/kimanipress

KPLITLSP